PLASTIC PLANKTON

A Pedro the Water Dog Saves the Planet Primer

AVIS KALFSBEEK

EXTRA FUN READS!

FREE DOWNLOAD

SHORT STORY PREQUEL

Hip-Hop Hope Slope

aviskalfsbeek.com/free

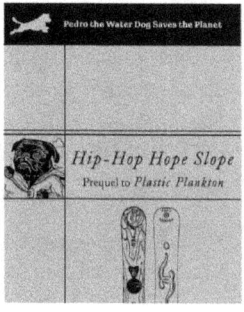

Acknowledgments:
Patron Patrons
Benjamin Katz Creative
Jaffe Lab at Scripps Oceanography, UC San Diego
Wallace J. Nichols, PhD, Blue Mind

ISBN 978-1-7355613-3-2 (First Edition Hardback)
ISBN 978-1-7355613-4-9 (First Edition Paperback)
ISBN 978-1-7355613-5-6 (Ebook)

www.AvisKalfsbeek.com

❧ Created with Vellum

For Timothy Moore and Jessie Elizabeth

CHAPTER 1

ACARTIA (ACANTHACARTIA) TONSA {CRUSTACEANS - COPEPODS - CALANOIDA}

Rock music blares out of a slightly opened window of a small cottage painted in bright, playful colors on the snow-covered shore of Lake Bijou Nez. On a winter morning in a modern time when many say the earth will eventually not sustain its humans, Camas, a strong young woman in her twenties, with curly strawberry blond hair, freckles, a fit, full-figure and one arm decorated in artistic tattoos, vigorously lifts her torso from a supine position on top of a paddleboard on the front lawn. Up and down. Up and down. She wears a colorful knit beanie and matching scarf, bright turquoise running tights, knit gloves, and a bikini top. She perspires from her enthusiastic workout, her breath creating rhythmic puffy clouds of condensation in the cold air as she lifts. However, she is not at all winded as she answers her phone. "What's up?"

"That's not a very warm welcome."

"I'm working out."

"By yourself?"

"Well, it would be with you, but you're traipsing around the islands without me."

"I'm training, not traipsing."

"Hmmm. What's that guy going to teach you?"

"That 'guy's' name is Liam," Tilly responds warmly. "We decided to focus on my swimming first, remember?"

Camas resumes her sit-ups, phone in one hand.

"Are you swimming a lot or kissing a lot?"

"I think both could help a training program."

"I knew it! You need to get back here!"

"Camas, what's up?"

Camas doesn't answer.

"Cam?"

"I miss you, damn it. I guess I'm a little jealous and feeling sorry for myself that I'm out shlepping the One More Year message alone."

"You're not alone."

"I'm doing sit-ups on your paddleboard on the front lawn in the snow because I miss you, and I'm going crazy here without you."

"What about the fin?"

"I took it off, of course."

"Kiss Josh, and I'll be home in a fortnight."

"How long is that?"

"Two weeks, silly. For the OMY unveiling in Spokane, duh. Thanks for running herd on that. Can't believe it's really happening."

"I didn't do much, sista."

"Yes, you did. Gotta run, and you need to work on your abs."

Camas looks down at her stomach.

"I miss you mucho," Tilly adds.

She is not able to see the tear in Camas' eye.

"I don't miss you." Water laps onto the snowy bank of the lake in front of the cottage as Camas continues her sit-ups.

The water sparkles as it blends into the shimmering warm water of an island in the Pacific.

CHAPTER 2

EUTERPINA ACUTIFRONS
{CRUSTACEANS - COPEPODS -
HARPACTICOIDA}

Lush tropical foliage and a waterfall surround the exquisite Hawaiian bay as Tilly swims ten yards ahead of Liam and her black curly-haired water dog, Pedro. Tilly's smooth dark hair looks like strands of long silk waiving like a dance in the tropical water. Pedro wears a doggy life jacket for their long-distance swims and is always happiest swimming next to his beautiful olive-skinned mistress.

Liam's strong, well-built arms and legs move in rapid quick motions to keep him afloat as he lifts his head to change course, his short curls dripping saltwater into his sparkling blue eyes. "Let's turn back!" he calls out to Tilly in his authoritative coaching voice.

Pedro barks in agreement as Tilly swims in a semi-circle to head back to the shore. Liam waits for them to pass and then puts his head down to swim with smooth strokes to follow.

The water-loving trio swims fifty yards further, and Liam lifts his head out of the water to call out, "Turn it on!"

Tilly swims faster as Pedro tries to keep up. Pedro begins to bark. Tilly looks back at him, then continues swimming. Pedro barks again.

Tilly stops again with a confused and disoriented look as she puts her hand to her head. She turns around to make sure Pedro is still swimming, then swims on.

Pedro barks again.

"P, no!" Liam scolds.

Tilly stops. "It's OK. He's trying to tell us something."

"Tell us what?"

"I'm not sure. It looks like he has something in his mouth. P, come!"

Pedro swims strongly to Tilly, his head raised with his find.

"Whatcha got, boy?" Tilly says in her lilting P voice.

Tilly treads water as she holds his lifejacket. With her other hand, she reaches to take something out of his mouth. She holds it up out of the water to show Liam as he swims to reach them.

It is a SodaCo-labeled plastic bottle.

"Good dog," Liam says as he tucks the bottle into Pedro's lifejacket. "Let's get home."

They begin swimming quickly until Pedro barks again, this time with more urgency. Tilly feels something lightly bump her head as she swims. Next comes the sensation of things lightly touching her arms. Liam stops abruptly, startled by the same.

Multi-colored plastic bottles and pieces surround them, bobbing in the water.

"Oh no," Tilly said as if in physical pain. She begins to cry.

Tilly and Liam hold each other for a moment, their feet treading in the deep water. Pedro comes up close with concern. Liam kisses her tears.

They feel water movement on their legs from two large sea turtles brushing past the love circle. Pedro swims to chase the turtles towards the shore.

CHAPTER 3

SAPPHIRINA SPP {CRUSTACEANS - COPEPODS - POECILOSTOMATOIDA}

A thirty-five-foot monohull sailboat cruises the northern Pacific Ocean off the coast of the Big Island of Hawaii in the bright mid-morning sun. Melodic hip hop thumps loudly as Moore, a slender young man with short dark hair and boyish handsomeness, stands confidently at the helm, wearing a ball cap, long shorts, white boat shoes, and a white polo with a unique front pocket. He moves his head with precision as he enjoys the sound of the waves crashing against the boat with the drop of the bass beat, the lyrics dancing with the koleas flying in the draft of the sail.

"Where we headed?" Spit asks as he walks out of the sailboat's cabin groggily wearing swim trunks and oversized sunglasses. His sandy blonde hair is disheveled and almost reaches his tan shoulders.

Moore bends over to unfasten the sheet to trim the mainsail.

"Same place I told you last night and, gee, thanks for standing watch, man...not," Moore says good-naturedly.

Spit looks confused. "And where was that again?"

"Not far from Hawaii, where the plastic island is floating."

"Got it. And we're going there because?"

"Spit, dude. I'll tell you *again*," Moore says as he rolled his eyes, "after you have some Joe and before the spinach."

"OK, where's the coffee?"

"Your mom stopped over and made it for you this morning. It's in the galley in your Ernie mug, next to your sippy cup."

"I can make the coffee," Spit says sheepishly, shaking his head as he walks down into the boat.

Josh, an athletic young black man with a beard, wearing a knit beanie, jeans, and a t-shirt with *IdaHome, where your life matters and my life matters* on the front, laughs as Camas chair-dances to a live bluegrass band while sitting on a barstool at Match-Love Brewery. Josh is in the close circle of Sandglass friends affectionately know as the Bike Guys for their love of mountain bikes.

"I love seeing your muscles under that shirt, handsome," Camas says, flirting.

"Thanks, Cam." Josh tries to kiss her dancing face.

Camas finally stops for the kiss. "I sent a note to Moore to come to the One More Year unveiling in Spokane."

Josh is surprised. "Do you think that's a good idea?"

"I know, I know. I should've asked her. It's just that this is a huge deal for Tilly, and I thought he should know.

"Why this?"

"I just felt it was time."

They turn to watch the band for a couple of minutes.

"Any response?" Josh asks.

"Not yet."

CHAPTER 4

PLEUROBRACHIA BACHEI
{TRANSPARENT - CTENOPHORES
- CYDIPPIDA}

Ember Ferry, a petite Asian woman in her late thirties, with short black hair in a ball cap, rides a vintage Dutch bike along the bustling Venice Beach bike trail. She passes swiftly by the colorful tourist shops, sidewalk artists selling paintings, and a musician with long dreadlocks playing a reggae tune on his electric guitar. She wears large headphones around her neck, Levi's with a wide cuff, red canvas deck shoes, and a T-shirt that says *Drink Better* on the front. Her pug, Plastic, sits happily buckled into the basket on the rear of the bike. Ember waves to people walking, skating, and biking past, and they return the gesture or smile and say hello to Plastic.

Plastic bottles lie at the foot of a trash can overflowing with trash and containers. She stops and picks up an empty WowFlo sparkling pomegranate plastic container, shoves it under her T-shirt, and continues riding.

Ember pedals two miles then crosses the street and rides away from the beach towards downtown Santa Monica. She stops and locks up her bike at a bike rack with close to one hundred colorful bikes, unfastens Plastic's bike harness, picks him up, and carries him into an ancient brick building.

Upbeat pop music and happy employees in open cubicles greet Ember. A large WowFlo logo is on the two-story wall of the high-ceiling space.

Ember nods to various employees as she walks quickly up two flights of stairs, skipping every other step with Plastic in her arms, to her executive office at the top.

Arthur, a skinny young man in a plaid short-sleeve shirt, skinny-tie, and large black square-framed glasses, stands at her desk, arranging papers and photos.

"Good morning," Ember says brightly.

"You have a plastic bottle in your T-shirt again," Arthur responds, as he picks up a file. "Picking up trash again?"

"There was so much, I couldn't get it all, but I grabbed this to look at all day."

"You have a million of those same bottles right here."

"But this one was a dirty piece of trash littering the sidewalk, eventually to be littering the river, then the ocean," she says passionately.

"Put a message in it?"

"Not funny."

"And you want to look at it... because?"

"To gaze on it and meditate on the fact that the only plastic I want to see on this planet in the future is this one," she says, lifting her pug in the air.

Ember puts Plastic down and places the plastic container on her meditation temple above the fountain, next to Guanyin.

CHAPTER 5

PHYSOPHORA HYDROSTATICA {TRANSPARENT - SIPHONOPHORES - SIPHONOPHORAE}

The sun is low in the afternoon sky as Spit exits the cabin looking sleepy from his afternoon nap. Moore is at the helm singing and dancing. Spit laughs and sings along to the hip hop lyrics.

"Hey, you're up from your nap. Early for you," Moore says, standing at the helm.

"You know I like my beauty sleep," Spit responds.

"More than you like to shower."

Spit sniffs his armpit. "Hey, I'm roughin' it."

"You're rough, all right. Grab me a beer."

Spit tosses Moore a beer, opens one for himself, and sits down as the boat sails below a colorful sunset sky.

"Hey, Camas texted me about something Tilly's doing in Spokane. Inviting me."

"Did you tell her you can't cuz you're out in the middle of the ocean?"

"Not yet."

"What's the thing?"

"Some environmental shindig. I guess it's kind of a big deal."

"Well, maybe you should congratulate her since you can't make it. Send flowers or something."

"You surprise me with your sophisticated etiquette, Emily Post."

"Emily who? Hey man, what etiquette? She's your sister. It's family."

Moore locks the wheel and moves quickly to take down the jib.

"Let's fish!"

Moore turns the boat directly into the wind to slow it and lowers the mainsail while Spit grabs two fishing poles, casts the lines, and puts them into the pole holders. They sit down next to the rods, enjoying the music and the cold beer.

"Charles Moore discovered the Great Pacific Garbage Patch in 1997," Moore says abruptly out of the blue as if struck by lightning. "That's more than twenty years ago. How are we going to turn the tide on the climate if it took us twenty years to put that plastic scoop up machine into the water."

Spit shrugs.

"Now, there are five trillion pieces of plastic in the ocean they say and not just one island of trash but five. Five trillion pieces. Five islands! One of those islands has trash so thick you can be Jesus fuckin' Christ and walk on top of water."

"I think it was Peter who walked on water, man."

"How in the world did you remember that?"

"Hey, is this about the plastic or your sister? Calm down. It's beautiful out here. You're slumpin' my fishin'."

Spit's line tightens. The rod bends.

"I've got a bite!"

Moore stands to help Spit work the fish. They laugh and grimace due to its strength. There are a few additional expletives as they reel it to the edge of the boat and pull the beautiful fish out of the water.

"Catch or release?" Moore asks with a broad smile.

"Release," Spit answers, smiling proudly. "He looks like a major stud. We've got enough Mahi Mahi stocked up."

They pull the massive fish into the boat, lift it to snap a quick selfie, then hold it down on the deck to remove the hook. Together, they raise the fish in the net and lower it back into the water. The fish takes a jubilant jump out of the water and disappears.

"Is that what we're doing out here?"

"I just have to see that scoop up machine. I need to see how it works. I signed a contract to use a material made from used plastic bottles. That jacket I showed you."

"Yup. It's a cool jacket."

"I want to see those bottles firsthand. I don't know why." His voice raises. "I just need to!"

"Jeez, OK, OK. Let's go see the contraption."

CHAPTER 6

JANTHINA JANTHINA {WITH SHELLS - JANTHINA - NEOTAENIOGLOSSA}

Tilly's mussed hair shines in the morning sun as she wakes up slowly on a queen-sized bed with white sheets on a veranda of an oceanfront Hawaiian cottage built in the 1920s. The porch has billowing sheer curtains and a potted palm tree covered in colorful Christmas glass ornaments, starfish, and shells. There is a basket in the corner full of presents. She looks at the empty place next to her in bed and gets up. Her body is lean and athletic as she walks in a T-shirt and boy short undies to the edge of the veranda.

Liam is on the beach, fiddling with something in the back of a kayak.

"Why aren't you still in bed?" Tilly calls loudly.

"Merry Christmas! Why are you still in bed?" he calls back.

"We ran fifteen miles yesterday in this humidity. That's why. Merry Christmas! What's the plan for the day? And where's P?"

"Whoops, I let him wander a bit. P!"

Pedro comes bounding down the beach path with Esme, a

white French bulldog with a pink Hawaiian print collar. Pedro has a Christmas bow on his collar.

"You rascal! Who's your friend?"

Tilly puts on a pretty skirt, walks out to them, and pets Pedro. She and Liam have a slow kiss.

"Til, after we have Christmas breakfast, kiss some more, and open presents, we're going to row to a place nearby that should be pretty similar to the Kona start. We can swim there. Well, *you* can, I mean." He smiles charmingly.

"I like that kissing part..."

Pedro gives Esme a cute bark.

"...but why are we way over here at this remote beach?"

"To keep you away from all of those lusting Ironmen guys, of course."

Tilly laughs as she pets Pedro.

"Don't you like it here?"

"It's idyllic. I might not leave!" Tilly answers.

Liam takes Tilly's hand and leads her back towards the cottage. "Come open your presents."

Pedro barks in agreement.

CHAPTER 7

PHACELLOPHORA CAMTSCHATICA {TRANSPARENT - SCYPHOZOA - SEMAEOSTOMEAE}

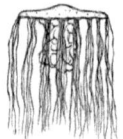

Several days passed in a Pacific Ocean hip hop mele montage of two friends heading to the plastic garbage patch on Moore's sailboat.

Moore draws in his sketchbook on the deck with Spit at the helm.

Spit does awkward pushups and dumbbell curls on the deck in shorts.

Moore and Spit talk as they lie on the outdoor boat seats, looking up at a star-filled night. There is a tiny artificial Christmas tree with lights on the bow.

Moore and Spit exchange small wrapped Christmas gifts. Moore opens his present, a book, *Cooking with Cannabis*.

Moore stands at the helm reading a book. Spit lies on the bow of the boat playing a video game.

Moore and Spit play beer pong on the galley table as they wait for fish, poles in the water.

Moore is making breakfast as Spit sits waiting for it at the table. They are rapping along to a song and laughing.

CHAPTER 8

DITRICHOCORYCAEUS ANGLICUS {CRUSTACEANS - COPEPODS - POECILOSTOMATOIDA}

Mr. Kunststoff, a tall, skinny, sixty-ish-year-old man with deep, dark circles under his eyes, talks on his cell phone in a large, modern, executive office with floor-to-ceiling windows and views of the city beyond.

"What do you mean, it's not picking up the trash?" Kunststoff shouts into his phone.

Christmas decorations adorn the cubicles in a huge office room with bustling workers on phones and computers, moving here and there.

A young man in the middle of the room answers Kunststoff. "Seems the trash is moving around the scoop-up apparatus but not capturing it. We're on it. Might need to get the machine to move faster, or..." He stutters. "...w...w...w... we have other ideas."

"W...w...w...well, figure it out," Kunststoff mocks, "god damn it!"He hangs up forcefully.

Sun streams through dramatic clouds as a sleek, modern, large catamaran sailboat with a French flag and full sails, white mainsail and red and blue jib, cuts through moderate waves. Hop Fillmore, a Frenchman of short stature, in his sixties with short grey hair and trimmed beard, stands at the bow. The boat on autopilot as he looks through vintage binoculars and sees another vessel in the distance.

"Sabine, slow to three knots," Hop says in his French accent.

The boat slows, and Hop walks to the helm. He pushes a button to turn off the autopilot and steers toward the other boat.

"Stopped. Hmmm. Fishing way out here. That's unusual." He speaks louder, "Sabine, locate the closest boat."

"Yes, sir. Searching," Sabine responds in a sultry French accent reminiscent of Bridget Bardot. "The closest boat is the Alkemia Earth. Three-quarters of a mile southwest."

"Merci, Sabine. I see her. Intriguing boat name."

"De rien."

Pedro plays with Christmas wrapping paper on the floor of Tilly and Liam's rental cottage. There are opened gifts on the couch, coffee table, and bed. Tilly answers her cell phone.

She listens.

"Merry Christmas to you too!"

"I didn't say Merry Christmas. I asked if you are running," Camas says, perturbed on the other end.

"Not yet."

"What?!"

"Kissing is more fun in the water."

"It's a triathlon, not Blue Lagoon! We're running first thing when you get to Spokane."

"Thank goodness. Miss you and love you. Merry Christmas!"

CHAPTER 9

BEROE FORSKALII
{TRANSPARENT - CTENOPHORES - BEROIDA}

"Hey man, there's a boat out there!" Spit points with food in his mouth.

"I've been watching it. An old man and a French Bulldog."

"What's he doing?"

"Can't really tell."

"Can you give him a signal?"

"What kind of signal?"

"Some kind of Morse Code flashlight shit. Like in the movies."

"We have a radio system, Einstein."

"What?"

"It's like a party line like our grandparents had for their phones in the old days. Only for boats. VHF, dude."

"Well, VHF the guy, man!"

"What should I say?"

"Cute Frenchie?" Spit says, laughing at his joke.

"Forget it. I've got it."

Moore picks up the radio and speaks loudly and confidently, "Alkemia Earth here. Are you safe and sound? Over."

"That sounded fuckin' nautical."

"Thanks."

Solemnly and silently, they wait, watching Hop's boat. There is no response.

Spit's eyes widen. "What if he's a pirate or some god damn psychopath out here preying on innocent boats in the middle of the ocean?"

Still no response.

"I'm sure if he were looking to prey on someone, he wouldn't be out here in the middle of nowhere."

Spit jumps out of his seat. "Where are the spears?!"

"You know where they are. Sit down."

The boat radio beeps. They hear a voice.

"Safe and sound, thanks. Hop Fillmore is my name, sailing the Ginette Neveu. OK to approach to say hello? Could use a beer if you have one."

"See, he likes beer, has a dog. He's good."

Spit still looks nervous. "Your criteria seem light."

"Moore DeMontagne and Spit Helena here. Beer on board. Over."

CHAPTER 10

PARAPHRONIMA CRASSPIPES {CRUSTACEANS - HYPERIID AMPHIPODS - AMPHIPODA}

Camas and Tilly run along a beautiful river trail. White water rapids rush far below with the Spokane city skyline shining across the expanse.

"I missed you, Cam."

"I didn't miss you."

"Yes, you did."

"Nope."

"Thanks for holding down the fort. One More Year is rockin', even without me."

"Especially without you. We don't need your tears and passion. We just need money."

Tilly laughs. "Probably right!"

"Kidding. Seriously, I want to tell you something important."

"You, serious?"

"An epiphany I had while having wild sex in the woods?"

"Really?"

"Kind of."

"What was it?"

"Well, Josh was stand..."

"The epiphany! Not the sex!"

"Oh, OK. Can I be honest with you about something?"

"I hope you're always honest with me."

"When you first started the Ironman, I didn't understand it. Yeah, I understood you're an amazing athlete. Well, almost as amazing as me." Camas smiles. "I understood that you wanted to do something new, learn to ride a bike fast. But I didn't understand if you loved Sandglass and your people so much, and the environment, why you would want to spend so many hours competing. It seemed selfish to me."

Tilly is surprised. "Thank you for being honest... I guess."

"And then I realized that your *why* has nothing to do with me. That wasn't easy because, well, I'm the self-centered one, you are my best friend, and we've been like Tom and Jerry, Lucy and Ethel, Scooby-Doo and Shaggy."

Tilly interrupts, "Wait, which one of us is Scooby-Doo?"

"Then I realized that I needed to make my own why out of it."

They run faster down the trail, turn down a city street and join in running with thousands of other runners, many in costumes.

Camas breathes heavily. "And my why for your Ironman is that I think we can take One More Year all over the country and the world. The planet isn't going to make it if people don't get out of their cars, like... forever.. to walk, bike, run..." She motions to the crowd of runners. "They also need to swim so they know they don't want to swim in a sea of plastic trash. People listen to your voice, Till. You've started a movement. We need to keep it going. I think we can make a real difference!"

Camas slows down and stops. She is breathing heavily and has tears in her eyes. She puts her hands on her hips. "We can't all run and swim and bike as fast as you, but we can be inspired by you. I'm inspired by you."

"Wow, you have been getting some really good sex. I'm inspired by *you*, sista'.

Tilly grabs her and hugs her strongly. "I knew you missed me."

"Solving the world's problems before breakfast. Check! Ruh Roh, it's getting late! Let's hurry and find some grub before the event!"

CHAPTER 11
ABRALIOPSIS FELIS {SQUID - SQUID - TEUTHIDA}

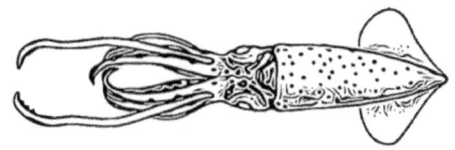

Hop's boat approaches. Esme, a white French Bulldog, is at the bow excitedly wagging her tail. The sails lower by themselves, and the vessel slows almost to a stop. Hop and Esme get into the dinghy.

"Sabine, keep a course close to Alkemia Earth. Lower the dinghy. Stand by for our return," Hop commands.

"Lowering dinghy. Enjoy your trip. Standing by."

The dinghy lowers to the water. Hop unhooks the cable, turns on the motor, and steers the boat with Esme pacing from side to side.

"Did you hear that? He's talking to his boat!" Spit says in a hushed, animated voice.

"It's OK, Spit."

Hop reaches the sailboat and quickly ties up. Esme climbs onto the edge of the dinghy, and Hop gives her a lift onto Moore's boat. Moore reaches out a hand to help Hop up.

Hop smiles warmly, "Thanks."

"Welcome aboard."

Esme barks a hello.

"Hope bringing the dog is OK."

"Sure."

"Esme, this is... Moore, is it?"

"Yes, and this is Spit," Moore responds.

Esme licks them both and then jumps down into the boat's cabin and disappears.

"Don't worry. She's pretty well-mannered. If there is food low though, she'll find it."

Spit looks alarmed and races to follow her.

"Esme!"

"He's just protecting her from his chocolate, I'm sure, and maybe some junk food and cannabis."

"Oh, good. Don't need a stoned Frenchie."

Moore and Hop laugh. Moore reaches into the cooler and hands Hop a beer.

Hop sits down. "Thank you. How are you two enjoying your trip?"

"Spit's my best friend from grade school. We don't always see eye to eye on things, but I know he's got my back."

"That's a good type of friend to have."

"Yup. I used to have that with my sister but..."

Spit bounds up the cabin steps with Esme in his arms.

"Found her! Just before she found a stash of malted milk balls."

"Happy you protected her from your *stash*," Moore teases. He turns to Hop. "We caught a Mahi Mahi today. Would you like to have dinner with us?"

"That would be nice."

Moore gets up and runs down into the cabin to prepare dinner. Spit puts Esme down. She has become his new best friend and sits lovingly on the bench next to him, looking at him as he speaks.

"That's a cool boat you have. It talks, huh?"

Moore exits the cabin with a platter of raw fish, salt, pepper, herbs de Provence.

"That's Sabine."

Spit gives a teasing glare to Moore, "We don't have a talking boat." He turns to Hop. "How'd *you* get that?"

"I made it...her, Sabine, myself."

"Wow. How?"

Moore nudges Spit.

"Be cool."

Spit is confused. "What?"

"It's OK. I worked with Steve Jobs when they bought the Siri technology. Later on some other voice robotics. I just thought talking to my boat would be easier and more fun so I gave it a try. She doesn't always abide."

Spit shakes his head. "Women."

Hop chuckles.

"You know about women? You boys seem too young."

Moore only thinks about his boat and drawing in his note-book. I know about women."

"What do you know about them?"

"I would get off this godforsaken boat if one liked me. I know that!"

"One doesn't yet, except your mother, so you're stuck with me."

Hop laughs. "Spit says you're drawing. What are you drawing?"

"I'm just writing some things and designing some clothes."

"Sounds interesting."

Moore seasons the fish.

"Why are you out here so far?" Hop asks.

"Mr. Fillmore..."

"Call me Hop."

"Hop, with all due respect, would you answer that first?"

Esme barks.

"Oui, but of course."

Esme runs to the bow of the boat and barks to the water.

"We're here to see le grand patch pacific garbage, the Great Pacific Garbage Patch."

Spit and Moore look at each other and raise their eyebrows.

"How close are we to it?" Moore asks excitedly.

"Pretty darn close, Sabine tells me. OK, your turn."

"We're here for the same reason. Or, I am, and Spit has agreed to keep me company. I told him there might be girls in bikinis on boats."

They laugh. Spit shakes his head and gives Esme a kiss on her head.

"I have a plan for a clothing company that uses all recycled materials. After I decided to use a material made from recycled plastic bottles, I had a dream. This may sound strange.

"I doubt it."

"Yes, it does." Spit rolls his eyes. "Go on."

I dreamt of a salmon that at the end of its 200-mile journey upstream in Alaska, amidst the flurry of spawning excitement and drama, it turned away, just before the end and a red-tailed hawk the size of a condor," Moore pauses, "Well, it was a dream... picked it up and put it into a river going back downstream. As it swam, so elated that it had tricked death with the help of the hawk, it came upon a river inlet. The inlet was filling the river with plastic. He turned back and found another inlet. Still more plastic filling the river. More and more and more. Unending water bottles and plastic pieces and plastic bags. Then I woke up."

"That is a powerful dream. What was it telling you?"

"That you had too many green teas and downward dogs this morning?"

Moore ignores Spit. "I don't really know, but it made me ask the question, where is all the plastic in the ocean coming from and how is one speck on top of the ocean, like Horton Hears a Who, going to make a difference? I read that every ten years, we're doubling the plastic we're putting into the ocean, and if it continues, plastic in the ocean will weigh more than fish."

"That sounds right."

Moore looks intently at Hop. "It's as though you're vacuuming your living room, and I'm standing in the doorway with a big bag of dust and a fan behind it. You can keep vacuuming, but you could never catch up. Like my dream."

"Good analogy, son," Hop says.

"It makes me think there might be something else going on with that scoop up machine. It just doesn't make sense."

"Damn, bro. Maybe you think the astronauts didn't land on the moon either."

"I just want to make sure the great plastic patch scoop up is legit. I didn't think it would take much to find out. Sail out there and check it out."

Esme pants heavily.

"Gentlemen, Esme is beside herself in joy here but I think I need to limit her excitement for one night. Thank you for the dinner invitation but I need to get back."

Moore and Spit look surprised.

"Will you join me instead, tomorrow evening? Spit, I'll introduce you to Sabine."

"Sounds cool."

"Esme, come."

Esme jumps into Spit's lap and kisses his chin, then runs and jumps into the dinghy. Spit grins, wiping off the wet dog kiss. Hop gets ready to step in, and Moore holds his arm to steady him. Hop stops, their arms straight, entwined, and turns to Moore.

"Young Moore, I'm here for the very same reason."

Hop turns away, steps into the dinghy, and sits down. He turns the ignition and motors back to the catamaran.

"See, he didn't murder us."

"Yet."

CHAPTER 12

NANOMIA BIJUGA
{TRANSPARENT -
SIPHONOPHORES -
SIPHONOPHORAE}

A huge crowd is celebrating at the finish of the famous annual Bloomsday run. Jubilant runners are gathered on the Monroe Street bridge in front of a stage with views of the Spokane skyline.

The mayor of Spokane, a pretty black woman with grey at her temples, wearing colorful running attire and a T-shirt with the words *Love Lives Here*, stands on the stage below a giant veiled billboard and speaks into the microphone.

"Congratulations, Blooms-day runners! Well done!"

The crowd cheers.

"Thanks for making the 44th Bloomsday a huge success. We have a surprise for you today. Local Sandglass triathlete, Tilly dementing, is here with us!"

Loud cheers from the crowd.

"Her personal campaign, One More Year, has taken off. She's launching 15 billboards in major cities across the U.S. over the next 12 months. This one above me is the first. Please give a big, loud Inland Northwest welcome to Tilly!"

The crowd claps, a Sandglass contingent is especially loud, and some chant, "Tilly!" "Tilly!"

Tilly runs onstage and shakes the Mayor's hand, then hugs her. The Mayor hands Tilly the mic.

"Hello, Bloomsday!" Tilly shouts.

The crowd cheers.

"Awesome job today! I'll keep this short, so you can start celebrating with that great Spokane beer!"

More cheering.

"Can you repeat after me?"

The crowd shouts, "yes!"

"Maybe a little louder? Can you repeat after me?"

The volume of the crowd's voices triples, "Yes!"

"We live on a tiny planet," Tilly shouts.

"*We live on a tiny planet!*"

"We don't need so much stuff!"

"*We don't need so much stuff!*"

The billboard veil slowly rises.

"Keep your stuff longer! One More Year!"

"*Keep your stuff longer! One More Year!*" the crowd booms.

Camas is at the edge of the stage and gets the crowd started chanting *one more year* as the billboard reveals, *OMY, One More Year. Keep your stuff longer, people*.

In the crowd, some runners wear OMY T-shirts.

"Thank you, everyone! I love you!"

A runner in the crowd shouts, "We love you, Tilly!"

Tilly gives the crowd a wave and her beautiful smile as she runs off stage and jumps with Camas to clap a high five in the air.

CHAPTER 13

LENSIA MULTICRISTATA {TRANSPARENT - SIPHONOPHORES - SIPHONOPHORAE}

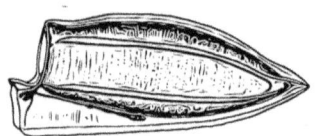

Moore steers a small dinghy toward Hop's boat as the sun lowers in the evening sky. Spit sits on the front edge of the boat wearing a vintage bowling shirt and long shorts.

"And we are going over to that old guy's boat because...?" Spit asks.

"Because he invited us."

"That dude is weird. Talking to his boat. Not staying for dinner."

"You're weird. Your girlfriend, Esme, will be there."

"She's not my girlfriend."

"She seems to love you. You should take what you can get. And thank god it finally got you to shower."

"Ouch."

Esme barks when she sees them approach. Hop comes out and gives a wave.

"Come aboard!"

Hop takes the painter line from Moore and ties the dinghy to his boat.

Hop's boat is much larger and newer than Moore's, a 60-

foot Gunboat Moonwave catamaran. The lower part of the boat is light blue, and the decor is French nautical with stylish touches like potted flowers and plants. There are a keyboard and a violin near the living room area.

"Come inside. Welcome!"

The boat's console is very high tech with two video displays in addition to his boat radar, weather, and radio systems.

"Wow. Cool gadgets!"

Esme jumps up on his leg and licks his hand.

"Esme, down," Hop commands.

"I don't mind," Spit says, petting her.

"What would you young men like to drink?"

"We brought some beer," Moore says, handing it to Hop.

"Would you like a martini first?"

"Sure," Moore and Spit answer in unison.

Spit tries to hide a smile as he says, "Shaken, not stirred."

Hop mixes three martinis. Spit and Moore try to look experienced when they drink but have trouble balancing their drinks with the slightly rocking boat. Spit gobbles up his olives. Hop leads them to the upper deck, where the table is set elegantly with fine china, silver, and more flowers. Moore and Spit's eyebrows raise, impressed by the table.

"Thanks for having us over," Moore says, holding his martini carefully.

Zara, an elegant silver-haired woman in her sixties, comes up the stairs with a tray of food.

"Gentlemen, this is my wife, Zara. Dear, this is Moore and Spit."

"Nice to meet you both," Zara says with a warm smile and French accent.

She sets the tray down to shake Moore's hand. Spit lifts her hand and kisses the air above it.

"Enchanté."

Zara smiles, and Moore rolls his eyes.

Zara motions to the table. "Please, sit."

Zara passes around a tray of grilled fish sprinkled with tiny edible flowers, a bowl of rice with vegetables, a dish of pistou, and a basket of warm bread. Hop opens a bottle of wine. Traditional French bistro music plays in the background.

The four eat dinner, laughing and telling stories about their boats, growing up, Esme, and Hawaii. The wine and the warm orange of the setting sun create a glow on the elegant table and their newly found friendship.

CHAPTER 14

CONCHOECIA MAGNA
{CRUSTACEANS - OSTRACODS - HALOCYPRIDA}

Tilly and Liam and the other passengers are greeted by two lovely Hawaiian women who put leis around their necks when they get to the bottom of the plane's exterior stairs onto the tarmac.

"I love Hawaii," Tilly says.

"We were just here and got leis."

Tilly hugs and kisses Liam. "I know. Isn't it great!"

"Can you please tell me again why my dad came with us?"

"Shush."

Graeme, Liam's father, and Camas exit the plane arguing about Tilly's training.

Graeme, a ruggedly handsome man, early-fifties with crows feet and short grey and blonde hair, speaks firmly, "She needs more cycling training."

"Her running isn't as strong as her swimming. We can't forget that."

"I'm not forgetting it. I just don't see her devoting enough time to cycling."

Liam turns around, speaking in a slow sing-song. "We can hear you."

Tilly smiles, "Hey, beautiful people, loves of my life, how about I alternate days with all of you. Camas running, Liam swimming, and Graeme cycling."

"That will work for this week. Then we can review what needs more attention as we get closer to the big day," Graeme says seriously.

"It's hotter than hell here. I'm not running in this," Camas complains, lifting her T-shirt to expose her abdomen to the air.

"Yes you are. We'll start at five am tomorrow morning," Tilly suggests.

"I'm the running coach. I'll set the schedule. I want to see some Big Island nightlife tonight. Let's start at seven."

"Seven it is!" Tilly laughs, shaking her head.

CHAPTER 15

LEPIDOP MYOPS {CRUSTACEANS - DECAPODS – DECAPODA

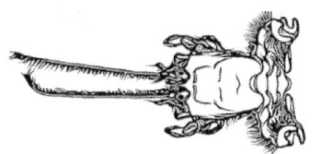

"So Hop tells me you're out here to see the plastic scoop up machine."

"That's right," Moore answers.

"You boys, be careful. We've seen some dangerous things out here."

"We've been told that. Thank you," Moore says respectfully.

"Abandoned boats or containers are a big hazard. As is this newfangled scoop up contraption."

Moore sits up straighter. "Have you seen it?"

"Are you finished eating?" Hop asks.

"Yes, thank you."

Spit shovels in a couple more bites. "Yes, I'm done too."

Hop stands. "Thank you, my darling, for the amazing dinner. Leave the dishes for me, please."

"Yes, it was delicious," Moore concurs.

"Thank you, Zara," Spit says.

Zara smiles warmly at the young men. "You're very welcome."

A little tipsy from the wine and martinis, the boys hold on

to nearby railings and furniture as they follow Hop down to the main cabin, then one more level down into Hop's office. It has a large desk with many nautical books, photos, marine gadgets, and on the wall is a large map showing the location of the garbage patches on the planet. The map also has some pins and post-it notes with annotations. He sits down at his computer. Moore stands behind him as Spit wanders slowly around the room, looking at the intriguing collection.

"I thought I might shorten the learning curve of your research if OK with you."

Moore is wide-eyed with enthusiasm. "That would be great!"

"You probably know that we're about 175 miles from their operation. Zara and I have been keeping a pretty close eye on it. We watch it from a NOAA satellite camera and when we're closer, with a drone."

"What's NOAA?"

"National Oceanic and Atmospheric Administration. They provide satellites to help keep an eye on environmental events. Besides the horribly disturbing climate data, we can watch the scoop up. I doubt they intended for it to help us zoom in on the machine, but it has been helpful."

Spit joins the group at Hop's computer. "Cool."

"I also have a good friend working for the Ocean Plastic Scoop Up Project, who has been keeping us updated."

"An insider spy?"

"They claim they're keeping the public updated on their progress, and I'm the public," he says with a sly smile. "I'm just getting more detailed and timely information."

"Like what?" Moore asks.

Hop brings up a video showing the machine. "Here's some live footage of it as we speak."

The boys lean in.

"You may have heard that it has had some trouble. What's

interesting, though, is that, although their website says they are diligently working to make adjustments to fix it, in actuality, they don't look to be doing anything." Hop points at the screen, "Look closely here."

Hop zooms in to an area in front of the machine. "What do you see?"

"I don't see anything."

"Exactly. No plastic. Maybe a bobbing milk carton here or a water bottle there, but no great mass o' plastic."

"Really?" Moore says, disappointed.

"There's more."

Hop clicks on a photo on his screen and expands it. It is a magical wonderland of mystical, fantastical, swimming zooplankton and phytoplankton swirling in a bubbly blue pool. Sparkling bright neon colors swirling and dancing.

"Wow, what's that?!" Spit asks, eyes wide.

"Those are plankton."

The wine-infused young men are mesmerized by the images.

"Plankton includes plants and animals that float along at the mercy of the sea's tides and currents. Their name comes from the Greek meaning *drifter* or *wanderer*. There are two types of plankton: tiny plants called phytoplankton and weak-swimming animals called zooplankton."

"They look crazy cool and psychedelic, man," Spit says slowly.

"No more wine for you," Moore teases.

"Here's the bad news. The machine is killing them. It's harming the plankton on the surface and other surface organisms that scientists call the neuston. The machine is churning along, killing it."

"What the fuck?" Spit blurts out. He is embarrassed, raises his hand to his mouth. "Whoops, excuse me."

"What the fuck is right," Zara says as she enters the room.

"The neuston feeds fish and whales in the ocean. It also contains baby fish who turn into very large fish."

"So, not only is it not cleaning the ocean, it's hurting the fishies? Why didn't these dudes figure that out in advance?" Spit asks.

"They claim they figured in the neuston and that the casualties are minimal," Hop says in a disapproving tone.

"Aren't they trying to fix it?"

"We're concerned that the scoop up machine may be just a fake attempt by some big plastic companies to appear environmentally correct. Just part of its propaganda that they have a conscience when in actuality, it is business as usual. Companies like NestTree and SodaCo, for example." Zara explains.

"SodaCo? I love cola," Spit says.

"Too many people love it," Zara says passionately. "Did you know that in some countries, cola is less expensive and more available than water? Besides causing extreme health problems like diabetes and obesity, SodaCo and its competitors are some of the biggest contributors to plastic pollution. C'est une catastrophe!"

"That totally sucks. I wanted to use plastic material for my designs."

"That's admirable," Hop says.

"What can we do?"

"We plan to expose it. We're just not sure how yet," Zara answers.

"Can you post some type of exposé online?" Moore suggests.

"My experience is that large, powerful corporations can get those things blocked pretty quickly."

"I still need to see it for myself."

If we sail about twelve hours a day, we can be there in

three days. Zara and I plan to get a neuston sample at the machine."

"We'll help," Moore says.

Spit turns to Moore, "Hey man, I want to get back to the girls in bikinis."

Hop hands Spit a Playboy magazine. Spit has a big grin, although he is a bit shy in front of Zara.

"Hope this can suffice until you're back, young man. I'll radio you tomorrow. Shall we depart at 600 hours?"

"Roger."

CHAPTER 16
ARCHICONCHOEDCIA STRIATA
{CRUSTACEANS - OSTRACODS -
HALOCYPRIDA}

Kunststoff walks quickly through the offices with his assistant, Sarah, a pretty, waif-like young woman in her twenties, with fair skin and wire-rimmed glasses. Her flowing bohemian-style skirt and scarves fly behind her, and her colorful stack of bracelets jingle on her slim wrist as she runs close behind, trying to catch him.

"I have the status of the scoop up machine," Sarah says quickly.

"Speak."

"They can't figure out why it's not gathering much plastic."

"What do you mean they can't figure it out?"

"Seems the velocity needed to capture the plastic is higher than the machine's capacity. And it's killing some marine life on the surface."

Kunststoff stops. "Forget the ocean muck! $20 million spent on that god damned thing, and it doesn't work?!"

"It is a prototype, sir."

"Prototype my ass. They assured me it would get the EPA and the government of my case. I signed that piece of shit agreement to recycle 100% of our plastic by 2030, and this was supposed to help. They're threatening some type of plastic tax if we don't clean things up."

"They're trying, sir."

"Shit scientists. God damned environmentalists!"

Sarah pulls a report from under her arm. "I have another copy of the Refill Project report. As you recall, sir, it would have the largest impact on those goals."

"You know I hate that project. Too expensive. It would cost us a billion dollars."

"That might be an exaggeration, sir. Even if the investment is high, the analysts told us that it pays for itself with higher profits by 2035. And it would stop plastic from entering the ocean in the first place."

"Are you contradicting me, Sarah?"

"No, sir. I'm your assistant and research arm."

"Stop pushing that piece of shit Refill Project!"

Kunststoff and Sarah step into the elevator alone. Behind them on the wall is a large poster of SodaCo-sponsored Ironman triathlete, Anika Jambes, a beautiful, black Belgian woman with an athletic amazonian build, wearing a SodaCo kit and holding an ice-cold SodaCo plastic cola bottle up to her mouth as she stands over a tri bike.

"WowFlo has a prototype of a refill station."

"Christ, Sarah. Give it a rest! I want to see a report on the scoop up machine showing the retrieval of a huge amount of plastic."

"But, it's not cleaning up a huge amount."

"Make up the numbers then. I need that report by Friday!"

The elevator door opens, and they exit. Sarah's face is solemn in a painful grimace.

"Yes, sir."

"And for Christ's sake, smile once in a while!"

CHAPTER 17

VELELLA VELELLA
{TRANSPARENT - JELLYFISH -
HYDROZOA: ANTHOATHECATAE}

Tilly is in her running clothes in the kitchen of her Hawaiian cottage. Pedro bounces around at her feet.

"P, wake Camas."

Pedro wags his tail, runs over to Camas' bed, and licks her face. Camas opens her eyes."

"P, well good morning," she says groggily. "I thought a Hawaiian prince was kissing me, and I was going to be queen of the islands."

"Aloha kakahiaka, sleeping princess. Time to get up and run. Here's a smoothie."

Camas puts on her running clothes taking a few drinks of her smoothie. They fill their hydration packs, including a pack on Pedro's back, jump playfully off the front porch and run down the beach trail, Pedro following behind.

"It's so hot and humid already," Camas wines.

"Yep."

"That's why you wanted to leave so early."

"Yep. How far today, coach?"

We're going to run ten miles along the beach trail. Liam

will pick us up and drop us at Palani Road to run the Queen Ka'ahumanu Highway. We'll run the toughest part of the course to the infamous Natural Energy Lab. About 18 miles total."

"Wow, you've studied up."

"Of course. I talked with some other coaches and read up on past races."

"I had no doubt."

They run fast and strongly.

"How's Josh?"

"Gorgeous, sexy, and fun. He and the Bike Guys are coming over for the race in about a week."

"That's so great!"

"I think you can win this Till. If you want to, that is."

"I want to."

"Damn. I'm sweating like a fat pig."

"You look beautiful."

"You must love me."

"I do."

CHAPTER 18

EVADNE SPINIFERA
{TRANSPARENT - CLADOCERANS
- DIPLOSTRACA}

I sland and ocean time pass as Tilly gains strength and speed, and the sailboats voyage onward toward the scoop up machine in a maile (MAH-ee-leh) makai (mah-KAH-ee) montage.

Zara plays the keyboard on the outside deck of the Ginette Neveu with Esme on her lap.

Graeme and Tilly ride their bicycles up a steep hill on the coastline with a volcano in the background.

Spit lies in the hammock *reading the articles* in the Playgirl Hop gave him.

Tilly and Camas run down a jungle trail listening to the same music on wireless headphones. Camas changes the song on her iPhone, and they stop and do a synchronized dance and then continue running.

Moore, Spit, Hop, and Zara are having dinner on the Ginette Neveu. Afterward, they play instruments and sing together, Zara on keyboards, Hop violin, Moore guitar, Spit shaker-egg percussion.

Liam paddles a kayak with Pedro in the front next to Tilly swimming in a beautiful Hawaiian bay.

Tilly and Camas hug the Bike Guys, Reeve, Josh, Cutter, and Joe, upon their arrival at the Kona Airport. Reeve, in his late forties, fit, with salt and pepper hair, carries his surfboard off the plane. Cutter, in his early 30's, with red hair and beard, is taller than the group at 6'2". Joe, early twenties with dark wavy hair and a close-cut beard, raises his hand in the shaka *hang loose* hand gesture, middle and ring fingers down. The other guys follow suit. The Bike Guys, athletic, outdoorsy, with a Pacific Northwest vibe, get leis from the airline greeter. Camas kisses Josh.

Spit swims near Alkemia Earth with Esme in a doggy life jacket. A dolphin jumps out of the water as Spit lifts Esme onto the boat steps.

Zara shows Moore how to operate the drone from their boat. Spit is startled but not amused when the drone lowers and sneaks up on him reading the Playboy. Moore and Hop laugh heartily together across the water.

Tilly, Camas, Liam, Graeme, and the Bike Guys ride fast on mountain bikes down a windy, technical jungle trail, laughing. The Bike Guys take a jump from a stunt in the jungle just before it comes out into a clearing with views of the ocean.

Tilly and Liam run along a volcanic mountain trail to reach Lake Waiau at the top. They stop winded, hands on their thighs. Liam picks up a stick to draw a heart in the dirt and points to the lake. It is shaped like a heart. They kiss.

CHAPTER 19
CARYBDEA MARSUPIALIS
{TRANSPARENT - JELLYFISH -
CUBOZOA: CARYBDEIDA}

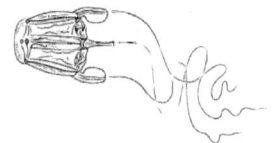

The handsome Bike Guys, wearing assorted vintage Hawaiian swim trunks and flip flops, wave as they ride up to the patio of a funky tropical outdoor café where Tilly, Liam, Camas and Graeme are sitting having an island spam, eggs and rice breakfast.

"Aloha, wahine nani. We're headed to the beach," Josh calls to Camas.

"Are you talking dirty in Hawaiian?" Camas calls back.

"I think so."

Camas walks to the edge of the patio and kisses him.

"Have fun, guys!"

Anika Jambes walks her bike between the cafe patio and the Bike Guys. The guys all turn their heads in unison to watch her. She is wearing a short running skirt, running shoes and a SodaCo cycling jersey, matching Italian-style cycling cap, and expensive racing sunglasses. Josh sees Camas with a stern look and quickly looks away from Anika. Anika does a double-take at the eccentric, athletic, handsome Bike Guys and then, without expression, continues walking.

"That's Anika Jambes, your top competition," Graeme says.

"She's tall," Tilly admires.

"Six two."

"She won Kona last year after winning four other Ironman competitions over the prior two years. Her sports are cycling, then running," Camas adds.

"Shit."

"She's fast, but so are you. She's dealt with this heat more, though," Graeme says.

"The planet and Hawaii are baking. I don't like it." Tilly pauses. "But, for this race, I can handle it."

"That's my girl," Camas and Graeme say in unison.

Camas and Graeme look perturbed, having said the same thing. Tilly smiles at her coaches.

"Tomorrow, we'll cycle the Chain of Craters Road. It has a good climb from the Kilauea volcano to the sea."

"Can we leave early?"

"I think Camas-time would be better for your training."

Camas nods her head in agreement. Liam shrugs.

"Darn."

CHAPTER 20

CLIO PYRAMIDATA {SHELLS - PTEROPODS - THECOSOMATA}

Moore and Spit sit across from Hop at his galley table. Zara stands at the helm.

"So, what's the plan when we get there?" Moore asks.

"We film as much as we can and hopefully take some samples of what's on the surface in the machine's path."

"How will we do that?"

"I've rigged up a robotic underwater camera," Hop says and places the camera on the table.

"Of course you have," Moore teases respectfully.

"It has a camera and the ability to bring back a sample if all goes well. Moore, you'll have your boat ready to leave quickly. Spit, can you make a boom for the camera? I think a fishing pole would do the trick."

"Will do."

"We should be there by tomorrow morning," Zara calls.

"Sounds good," the young men say in unison. They smile and raise their glasses of beer.

Hop and Zara raise their glasses of wine.

"Cheers!" Zara calls.

"Cheers!"

Sarah's cubicle is decorated with a 1967 Janis Joplin Jefferson Airplane at Winterland poster with a large peace sign and a white dove on the top of it, a photo of her parents, and a fluffy white unicorn cat greeting card. She dials the phone.

"Rob Prend, please."

Sarah taps her pen on the desk, waiting. She looks worried.

"Hey Sarah, what's up?"

"Things are moving along. Kunststoff wants a report of the plastic retrieved from the machine."

"We've had problems."

"He told me he doesn't care. He wants a report that you've captured plastic. Significant plastic."

"Shit."

"Yep."

"We got some bad press."

"I heard."

"So, I don't think it's good timing to make up that we've collected a lot of plastic when we haven't."

"What do I tell Kunststoff?"

"Tell him to pull that plastic out of his ass."

"I don't think that will go over well."

"Sorry, Sarah. Can't help you."

"Thanks anyway, Rob."

Sarah stands up and puts down the phone. She mimes pulling something from her derriere into the sky, like a magician pulls scarves out of a top hat. She chuckles, then looks worried again.

CHAPTER 21

CHRYSAORA COLORATA
{TRANSPARENT - JELLYFISH -
SCYPHOZOA: SEMAEOSTOMEAE}

Spit assembles a boom for the underwater camera on the edge of the boat.

Moore picks up the radio. "Alkemia Earth to Ginette Niveu."

"Copy."

"I see it! Looks about two miles out?"

"There's a good chance the boat crew isn't keeping a close watch." Hop's voice comes over the radio speaker. "We'll sail over and then send Spit in the dinghy with the camera and take the samples. Over."

Spit looks up from the table, "I'm on it, but how fast is the machine moving?"

Moore puts the radio back up to his mouth, "Spit wants to know how fast the machine's moving."

"It's drifting with the ocean currents, so between two and three miles per hour. Over."

"Does he go inside the net?" Moore asks.

"Outside only. We don't want him getting caught in the net, and if we run into any trouble from the crew, I want to get him out of there quickly. I'll run the drone close to the surface, but the photos might not be clear enough,"

"I'll get the underwater shots," Spit says, threading a wire through the fishing pole guides.

"He'll get the underwater shots." Moore tires of translating. "Get over here, MacGyver."

Spit gets up and takes the radio. "Hey Hop, I'll get the underwater shots, sir.," He pauses, thinking, "Hey, I just thought of something. How am I going to steer the dinghy?"

"Zara is going to drive for you. She'll pick you up when we're closer."

"Roger that. Over and out."

Moore looks serious. "Are you sure you want to do this?"

Spit puffs out his chest.

"Buddy, I was born to do this."

CHAPTER 22

CLYTIA LOMAE {TRANSPARENT - JELLYFISH - HYDROZOA: LEPTOTHECATAE}

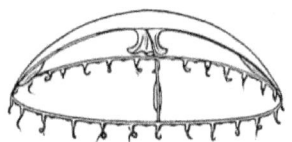

Ember and Plastic ride down the beach trail on the way to work. Plastic has his ball cap on backwards. Ember's phone rings and she stops at a traffic light to answer. "Good morning."

"I got a call from SodaCo that I thought you'd want to know about," Arthur says.

"Kunststoff called?"

"No, it was his assistant. Her name's Sarah."

"Oh, yeah. I remember her. We talked at FoodEx in Japan. She seemed spunky."

"She might be spunky, but she sounded desperate. It seems SodaCo is in a pickle. They're sponsoring that ocean scoop up rig, and it's having problems. She wants to meet with you."

"Why?"

"She didn't give me any more details but just said it's of critical importance. She lives in Chicago and is hoping you can come to her."

"I'll do it. Set it up, please."

Tilly knocks on the door of Graeme's Kona condo. He doesn't answer. She knocks again, then opens the door.

"Graeme?" Tilly calls.

Still no response. She walks in and sees him asleep on the couch.

"Rise and shine, sleepyhead," Tilly says gently with kind eyes.

Graeme wakes. He sits up quickly, embarrassed.

"Tilly, good morning," he says groggily. "Sorry. I must have fallen asleep studying the course last night after I took half a pain pill for my back."

Tilly sits down next to Graeme. "Are you sure you're OK to ride with me?"

Graeme smiles. He gives her a gentle push on her shoulder. "Hey, you're just afraid I'll outride you."

Tilly laughs. Graeme walks into the bedroom to change.

"My life would truly be over if you start feeling sorry for this old man and his aches and pains," Graeme says from the other room, changing into his kit.

"I don't."

Graeme walks out, pulls his cycling shoes on. Grabs his gloves and helmet. "Good. Let's ride!"

CHAPTER 23

CLAUSOCALANUS ARCUICORNIS
{CRUSTACEANS - COPEPODS - CALANOIDA}

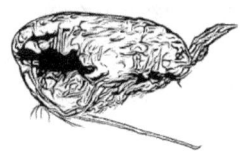

The mid-day sun shines brightly on the two sailboats as they approach the plastic scoop up machine. Its large U-shaped barrier has a net-like skirt that hangs below the surface of the water and surrounds a commercial-sized tug boat equipped with a crane arm to pull plastic out of the water, had it been capturing any. One crewman sleeps in his cabin below deck and the other in the wheelhouse chair, open mouth snoring.

Zara brings the dinghy close to the apparatus. Spit extends the boom and drops the camera down into the water inside the scoop barrier. The waves cause the camera to bounce up and out of the water and, despite having practiced, Spit finds it impossible to control the boom. He can't get the camera to hold position long enough for the shots, or to gather the specimens. Zara keeps the boat close. She sees Spit struggling.

"I can't get the camera close enough!"

"Mierde!"

Spit quickly pulls off his shirt, takes the camera off of the long pole, and fastens the strap around his wrist.

"Spit, no. C'est tres dangereaux."

"It's the only way. Get me as close as you can!"

"Use les palmes!"

Zara drives the dinghy closer and bumps the barrier as Spit pulls on the fins.

Spit dives over it to the inside. He gives Zara the thumbs up, takes a deep breath, and dives down under the water towards the skirt on the face of the curved barrier.

Waiting on the boats, Hop looks at Moore across the water and raises his hands upwards as Moore shakes his head in disbelief.

"Hey, you, what are you doing? Get away from there!!" The crewman shouts from the deck.

CHAPTER 24

OITHONA NANA {CRUSTACEANS - COPEPODS - CYCLOPOIDA}

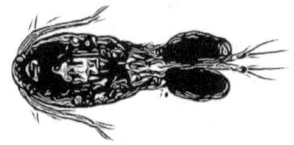

Insightful determination weaves an inland mauka (møyːka) mountain montage.

Sarah searches through a file cabinet in the SodaCo offices. She finds a copy of the Refill Project report and puts it into her bag.

Graeme and Tilly ride fast over beautiful rolling hills in a tropical rainforest. The lush, misty green foliage is in stark contrast to the next miles through the Ka'ū Desert. They pass dried lava, volcanic ash, and gravel in the oppressive heat.

Ember is on her laptop at a hip Venice Beach café with Plastic lying on the seat next to her. She researches SodaCo corporate stockholder reports.

Zara hugs Spit as she drops him back at Moore's boat. Spit climbs onto the Alkemia Earth. Moore gives him a hive five and hugs him strongly. Hop gives them an enthusiastic thumbs-up, then a wave. Moore turns the boat to head back.

Ember lands in Chicago and exits her flight with a backpack, stretch pants, and tennis shoes. She grabs a bike from the city bike-share rack and rides along Lake Michigan with one headphone in, smiling and frequently stopping to pet dogs. She stops to take her cell phone out of her backpack and texts, *Sarah, meet me on the corner of Michigan Avenue and Wacker.* Ember continues riding along the water then turns onto a street towards downtown.

CHAPTER 25

ATLANTA PERONII {SHELLS - HETEROPODS - NEOTAENIOGLOSSA}

Tilly and Pedro swim in moderate waves along a stretch of Hawaiian coast as Liam paddles in a two-person kayak. She swims by quiet tropical inlets and by Ironman fans to whom she gives a smile and a wave, and P gives a bark. She swims strongly, then raises her head.

"Aren't we finished yet?" Tilly shouts.

Pedro barks.

"200 meters more. Push it!"

Pedro puts on extra effort and swims to Tilly's side. Tilly looks up and smiles at him. She puts on the extra push, and together they swim the last stretch."

Tilly rests her head on her hand on the kayak.

"Tomorrow, I want the kayak."

She kisses Pedro in the water, then kicks to rise to kiss Liam.

"How'd I do?"

"Great, baby. How'd you feel?"

"I got a little bored. I miss the lake with the mountains watching over."

"How do the mountains make it less boring?"

"Because I talk to them."

"When you're swimming?"

"Yeah."

Liam pulls Pedro up into the kayak, then reaches down with both arms and puts his hands on either side of Tilly's face and leans down with his face close.

"That is just another reason why I'm in love with you."

Liam pulls Tilly up into the kayak onto his lap, and they have a sweet kiss.

"Am I squishing you?" Tilly asks.

Pedro tries to squeeze between them.

"I like squishing."

They kiss again. Pedro barks.

"Till, I've meant to tell you something."

"What is it?" Tilly asks curiously.

"Moore's here. Well, not here, but in Hawaii."

Tilly is startled. She speaks quickly, "How do you know? Did you see him? Did you talk with him? Why didn't you tell me?"

"I'm telling you now. And I'm sorry. Remember the French Bulldog on the beach?"

"Yes."

"When you were out on the run yesterday, her owner was walking her on the beach in front of the house. We started talking. His name is Hop. Seems he does a lot of sailing around here and met Moore sailing off the coast recently. I'm not sure how I realized he was talking about Moore. I think it's when he said he met someone who designed clothes from plastic."

"What's he doing in Hawaii?"

"He didn't say. He's with a friend, though."

"What are the chances that Moore's here?"

"I got his number. Want to call him?"

"No. I've called him a trillion times."

"Maybe this time will be different."

Tilly pets Pedro but doesn't answer. Liam paddles to turn the boat around and back to shore.

CHAPTER 26

CLIONE LIMACINA {SHELLS - PTEROPODS - GYMNOSOMATA}

Tilly and Graeme ride up a very steep hill on the coast with dramatic volcanic rock on one side, ocean waves, and rock formations on the other. Their faces look in pain as they climb, but they are relentless, pushing and pushing, standing on their pedals to make it to the top.

They stop, sweat dripping down their faces, looking out over the Pacific as a tiny dot of a sailboat in the distance approaches the island. The breeze cools them as they drink from their water bottles.

"Sometimes I feel smaller than that speck of a boat on the sea. Like I might just fly off of the hill into the sky, never to be seen again," Tilly says wistfully, still catching her breath.

"A sad feeling?" Graeme asks gently.

"A temporary melancholy, yes."

"I get that. For me, it seems like I remember a past that begins before I was born."

Tilly continues gazing out to the sea. "Are you sure you aren't Native American?"

Graeme smiles. "Practically speaking, this strong breeze is

66

what you'll need to maneuver in the race. Spiritually speaking, you *are* a speck. But you are one hell of a fast, strong, speck."

Tilly laughs.

"Going down, I want you to practice keeping the required forty foot no draft length behind me."

"I'm going to pass you."

"No, I don't want you to pass. Now, or in the race."

"Why not?"

"Because you won't gain that much time and it's dangerous at those speeds."

"Teach me how to pass."

"No passing."

Tilly puts her hands on her hips and raises her voice, "Tell me, unless you want me to be disqualified."

Graeme lowers his head. Reluctantly, "You could read it in the rulebook, so I guess I'll tell you." He pauses, thinking. "You need to complete the pass within thirty-five seconds."

"OK."

Graeme speaks firmly, " No, not OK. That means you're forty feet back and need to be able to make up that forty feet and pass in thirty-five seconds."

"Got it."

"Tilly, it's just a race."

"Someone told me that would never be true."

The two take off down the hill, riding very fast, Tilly forty feet behind Graeme.

CHAPTER 27

CYPHONAUTES LARVAE
{INVERTEBRATE LARVAE}

Tilly enjoys the fresh ocean breeze sitting on the veranda of the Kona cottage. Esme runs onto the beach in front of her. Pedro races out when he hears Esme's bark. Hop approaches as the two dogs play in the waves.

"Good morning!" Hop calls and waves.

"Good morning!" Tilly smiles and calls back.

Hop walks closer to the veranda.

"Those two sure like to play together."

Tilly stands. "Yes, they're adorable."

"I'm Hop Fillmore," Hop says, extending his hand.

"Nice to meet you. We met Esme a couple of weeks ago."

"I stopped by because I'd like to invite you and Liam to a luau this evening."

"Oh goodness, that sounds great, but I don't think a luau is in my training meal plan."

"I've been seeing all of the calories you've been burning swimming. I don't think a bit of pineapple, roast pork and poi is going to hurt you... might even do you good."

"I have my Sandglass friends in town this week."

"Please, invite them all!"

"There are seven of us total. Nine with Liam and me. Hop, that's too many for you to pay for."

"There aren't many things I can do with too much money. Money can't buy me happiness or make me 21 again, or strong enough to do an Ironman, but it certainly can buy eleven seats at a luau. My wife, Zara, will be there too. Please accept."

"That sounds lovely."

"I'll pick you and Liam up at six. Pedro can come too. Tell your friends to meet us at the Waikoloa at 6:30."

"We'll look forward to it."

Hop walks towards the beach and calls to Esme, "Esme, let's go!"

"P, come!"Pedro reluctantly leaves Esme and runs onto the lanai. Hop turns around to wave, then walks back down the beach.

CHAPTER 28

BARNACLE LARVAI
{INVERTEBRATE LARVAE}

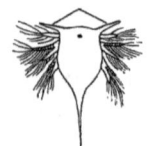

The Bike Guys grab wave after wave at Banyans as though they lived on the island, not in the high elevations of Sandglass. Each, an athlete in their own right, has spent months, and some years, of their past finding surf while waiting for the snow to ski, or just seeking to experience Hawaiian waves bringing time to a halt. Today was such a day.

A 1963 Ford Country Squire Woodie station wagon pulls into the beach parking lot with a surfboard on top. Ike, in his mid-sixties, grey-bearded, with tan leathery skin and tattoos, pulls an old-school longboard out of the van and strips down naked to pull on vintage swim trunks, then heads for the beach with his board. The Bike Guys sit on their boards waiting for him and give whoops and hollers as he paddles up. The good friends duck-dive out to find the best wave.

Ike embraces the surf like a long lost lover, carving a roundhouse cutback, followed by a floater. His wild all-out body antics cause the guys to laugh as they watch his humorous whacky surf moves.

The Bike Guys and Ike walk out of the surf with their boards.

"So great to see you, man. I thought you couldn't make it?" Josh says, shaking Ike's hand and hugging him.

"I thought I couldn't, but I met an old lady who fell in love with Suerte, and she told me I should go."

"Your new girlfriend?"

"Maybe," Ike says mysteriously. "Anyway, I'm here."

The guys laugh, and the others hug Ike too.

"I couldn't miss seeing Tilly compete."

"No kiddin', bro!" Josh agrees.

They get to Ike's woodie wagon and their rental rig. Josh's phone rings.

"Hey, Cam."

"How's the surfing, gorgeous?"

"Gnarly. The Benny's ripped it today. We totally attitude danced the motion of the ocean."

"Where are you?"

"Babe," he admonishes. "You know the first rule of surfing is never to tell anyone where you go. Ike's here, though!"

"Oh, that's right. Tell Ike, hi! Guess what? We're all invited to a luau. Some rich French guy's treating."

"Sweet!"

"I'll text you the info. Tell the guys."

The guys pull off their wetsuits and rinse off.

"Some hula girls, fire, and BBQ pork for you tonight?" Josh calls.

"Yeah!" they answer in unison.

CHAPTER 29

RHINCALANUS NASUTUS
{CRUSTACEANS - COPEPODS - CALANOIDA}

Hop, Zara, the Bike Guys, Camas, Tilly, Liam, and Ike are seated watching luau dancers as the sun sets. Their table is full of tropical flowers and Hawaiian delicacies. Pedro bounds across Waikaloa beach in front of the crowd, who are jubilantly enjoying the extravagant experience. The male dancers are singing and shaking energetically to the ancient rhythms. They finish, and female hula dancers begin moving their hands and gently swaying their hips to a slower song, matching the movement of the waves behind them.

"Ike, I'm so happy you're in Hawaii," Tilly says, hugging him.

"How could I miss it?"

"This music makes me miss Frida."

"She, Bear, and all of Sandglass miss you too. We're all with you."

"I know that."

They watch the dancers for a few minutes.

"Hey, where's P?" Liam asks, looking around.

"Shoot!"

"I'll go look for him," Liam offers.

"No, that's OK. It's my turn. I need to stretch anyway."

Tilly walks towards the beach through the crowds. She looks in either direction and then sees Pedro knee-deep in the water being pet by a tall, lanky young man, Moore. Tilly gasps.

Moore doesn't see her as she walks towards him. Spit is walking nearby, looking at the pretty girls in the crowd and the sexy hula dancers. Moore looks up and sees Tilly. Tilly immediately runs at full speed and stops in front of him, throwing her arms around him in a firm hug, her head on his chest. Moore's body is a bit rigid, but he settles into her hug and closes his eyes.

Tilly steps back and looks up at him. "I heard you were here. I didn't believe it."

"I'm here. I like your dog."

"This is P. I think he knew you without knowing you."

"Maybe."

"How are you?"

"I've been good. Sailing and exploring."

"That sounds nice."

"I hear you've been competing."

"Yep. Not really sure how it all happened."

"Seems natural to me."

Moore pets Pedro.

"Can you join us?"

"I've been invited," Moore says.

Tilly smiles, shakes her head in disbelief. "Of course."

The two walk carefully in unison, their footprints in the sand. A sweet traditional Hawaiian melody starts as they walk past a statue of Koleamoku with a kolea bird on his head.

"Cool statue," Moore says.

"The kolea bird is revered here because they are believed to be an incarnation of Koeamoku, the god of the art of healing," Tilly says as she holds Moore's arm to guide him behind a large palm tree.

Tilly has tears in her eyes. "I'm so sorry. I was so worried when you left and couldn't get a hold of you. I heard rumors that you weren't well, but I didn't know how to help you."

She takes his forearms in her hands and turns them upward. The skin is smooth and unmarked.

"Yeah, it's OK. I just stopped eating for a while."

"Oh, goodness."

"But Spit found me somehow in my hole-in-the-wall apartment in L.A. He dragged me out and told me to snap out of it and either start eating on my own or he was going to make me eat a potent strain of munchies pot."

They laugh.

"I see you're wearing your locket," Moore says.

Tilly puts her open hand on the locket and her heart. "Yes."

"Can I see it?"

Tilly looks down, opens it. Moore reaches out to touch it, looks closely at the two photos inside. Closes it. Tilly hugs him fiercely, and they walk arm in arm to join the group.

The music turns faster and louder. The Bike Guys know Moore as a kid growing up in Sandglass and shake his hand and hug him. Camas gives Moore a big hug and kiss. Hop shakes his hand with a smile. Spit walks up with Esme. He has wide eyes and a big grin as he points to the hula dancers.

"Tilly, you remember Spit."

Tilly smiles and gives Spit a strong hug.

Spit and Moore walk around to greet Hop and Zara.

"You're looking handsome, gentlemen," Hop says, extending his hand to Spit.

"Thanks for the cool invite!" Spit answers, shaking his hand.

Hop shakes Moore's hand. The boys lean down and kiss Zara on the cheek.

"How did the sample come out?" Moore asks.

"Brilliantly. Wonderful work," Hop answers. "We'll look at it together at my beach house.

"I tell you what. Besides what I scooped, I could see a bazillion tiny mystery shapes on the screen down there," Spit says enthusiastically.

"I don't doubt it."

CHAPTER 30

HETEROMYSIS ODONTOPS
{CRUSTACEANS - MYSIDS - MYSIDACEA}

The towering city skyline surrounds Sarah and Ember sitting together on the First Lady tourist boat on the Chicago River. A guide describes the buildings in the background as Sarah passionately speaks about SodaCo and Ember types notes into her phone, nodding her head.

The riverboat passes Marina City with its 1960's modern honeycomb circular towers, the luminous white beacon of the Wrigley Building, whose bell tower was styled after the Giralda Tower of the Seville, and the Tribune Tower, whose creation emerged from a contest to build the world's most beautiful building, a cathedral for journalism.

People on the boat hold plastic containers of soda, juice, and health drinks. Beer is served in red plastic solo cups.

Busy Chicago neighborhoods with shoppers dump plastic containers in the trash, and crowds cheer loudly across the city as the Chicago Cubs play the Saint Louis Cardinals at Wrigley Field.

"You can't see it from the boat, but just north is the famous Wrigley Field, home of the Chicago Cubs." The guide's voice trails off. There are thousands of plastic bottles in the spectators' hands, and trash receptacles at the stadium are overflowing onto the ground.

A local Chicago dumpsite has mounds upon mounds of plastic trash.

Ember lifts her head to listen to the guide. "The Cubs were originally the Chicago Whales..."

A burst of seawater shoots into the air from a whale blowhole swimming near the plastic scoop up machine. The whale disappears underwater.

CHAPTER 31

CESTUM VENERIS
{TRANSPARENT - CTENOPHORES
- CESTIDA}

The Ironman approaches as Tilly and Anika dig deep for their Kona koa (koh-uh).

Anika's face shows fierce determination as she rides a stationary trainer bike in a stark white workout room, watching a large screen of a hilly bike path in front of her, her coach standing by.

Tilly runs intensely through a tropical jungle trail with Pedro and comes upon a pool under a waterfall. The two run and jump into the water with splashes.

Anika runs on a treadmill in front of an ocean view in her modern beach condo. She stops running to answer her cell phone. Kunststoff's name is on her screen. She looks impatient and annoyed as she speaks.

Tilly swims the Kona course with Pedro, Graeme, and Liam in a kayak beside her. She runs out of the water and transitions to her bike. Tilly laughs as Pedro jumps out of the kayak and runs after her.

Anika swims in an indoor pool with triathletes swimming in the other lanes. Her four coaches stand on either end of the pool.

Tilly cycles along a coastline road catching up with a group of male cyclists going very fast. She keeps up with them. They smile at her strength and agility. Tilly turns onto another road, and the guys shout out, "Good luck, Tilly!"

Anika is on a massage table in the living room of her condo, having an intense, rolfing-style, massage.

Tilly does a beautiful vinyasa-flow yoga with Liam, Camas, Graeme, and Pedro on the beach outside her cottage.

CHAPTER 32

PTYCHOGENA SPP.
{TRANSPARENT - JELLYFISH - HYDROZOA: LEPTOTHECATAE}

Ember sits in her modern executive office with colorful images of fruit and clear sparkling water in streams behind her on the wall. Plastic lies under her desk. Arthur walks in with a brisk step.

"How was your meeting?"

"It was good. Smart girl in a shit company. When it started 130 years ago, it probably didn't plan to be shit, but now it's shit."

"Sugar kills people. Plastic kills fish. We're fossil fuel *fudged!*"

"She knows they're covering up their bullshit ocean scoop up machine."

"Really?"

"She asked me if we would collaborate with SodaCo on our refill initiative, or be competitive enough to pressure them to pursue theirs."

"Wow, yes, she is smart."

"I worry about her there."

"Hire her."

"She has more to do."

"What did you promise her?"

"Only that our project will stay on track. That we won't slow down." Ember pauses. "But I have another idea."

"You go, boss."

Celebrities in sunglasses and other fashionable customers sit on the sunny patio of the Hollywood Chateau Stairmont. Ember sits with California Governor Nevin Handsome, Plastic lying at her feet with a bright neon orange and pink dog bowl that says *Pug Love*. The governor is in his early fifties with a touch of grey in his combed back full head of hair and wears a grey suit, light blue shirt, and a dark navy tie. Ember sets her cell phone into a stand on the table and touches the screen. Sarah appears.

"Sarah, hi."

"Oh, hi! Wait. I need to find another place."

Sarah leaves her cubicle and rushes down a hall out the door onto a small balcony. "Thanks for calling."

"Of course. I've been thinking about our last conversation, and I'm here with a friend of mine."

Ember shifts the phone so Sarah can see both of them.

"Governor, this is Sarah. Sarah, Governor Nevin Handsome."

"Wow?!" She speaks awkwardly, "Uh, hello, so nice to meet you, governor."

"Sarah, the pleasure's mine. Ember has told me about the refill initiatives that SodaCo and WowFlo are working on. I'm sorry that your company seems to have stalled on that project."

"Yes, sir. It's a travesty."

"Travesty is a good word. It seems to be anti-environment corporations' modus operandi to create organizations that appear to be doing good as a public relations diversion. Similar to your SodaCo's scoop up machine, the organization *A Plastic Bottle's Life* sponsors Elementary School happy recycling contests, build a fantastical dragon to eat those nasty plastic bottles. In actuality, they are the PR arm of National Plastic Alliance, a lobbying group that fights restrictions on plastic and primarily made up of fossil fuel giants."

"They don't want change, that's for sure."

"I'd like to help."

"How's that?"

"I gave Jeff Mesopelogic a call. He's the..."

Sarah interrupts, "U.S. Senator from Oregon."

"Yes, that's right." He smiles and nods at Ember, impressed by Sarah's knowledge.

"He already has a bill submitted, and he's open to looking at some amendments."

"With all due respect, sir. I think the honorable Mesopelogic and his co-sponsors, while well-intentioned, are missing the mark."

Governor Handsome is surprised. "What do you mean? I thought you would love that bill."

"*The Break Free From Plastic Pollution Act* misses one huge thing."

"What's that?" Ember asks curiously.

"What if the margins on the drinks and water are so large, and they are, that these restrictions don't halt any production of plastic?"

The Governor and Ember look shocked.

"Think about it. This bill puts the cost of recycling on the beverage producers."

"Exactly."

"But, if they can absorb the cost, it's just a bee buzzing around their head. They'll swat at it, pay the taxes for the plastic, maybe raise some prices. We'll have a more organized method of accumulating the plastic at the state containment centers they propose, but it will still be an unending monstrous flow of plastic." She pauses. "And we all know that eventually, with the power of the fossil fuel companies, they'll whittle away at the regulations until we're back to square one!" She says passionately.

"Shit," the Governor says.

"We need a change in consumer behavior. We need to eliminate plastic containers altogether and train people to live in that world. That's what the bill needs to do. And tax the companies until the containers are at zero!"

"So, you would ask Senator Mesopelogic to submit a bill to Congress that would require all beverage companies to move to 100% refillable products by a certain date..."

"2030," Sarah interjects.

"... and applies a tax on them until then."

"Yes."

"Ember tells me you have an idea for a slogan to support consumer awareness."

"Yes, sir."

"Can I hear it?"

Sarah suddenly becomes shy.

"It's Refill, Bill exclamation mark."

"Who's Bill?"

"He's going to be the superhero that stops all this plastic."

Plastic wakes up under the table sleeping.

Plastic the pug runs along the beach in a superhero cape picking up plastic.

"It's perfect," the governor says.

Sarah smiles.

"If we can get him to submit it this week, we hope to announce it at the Ironman in Kona. We're trying to sponsor triathlete, Tilly De Mont...."

Sarah gasps, "I love Tilly! Sorry to interrupt again."

"That's OK. Tilly is expected to win, and if she does, she might agree to use the podium to promote the bill."

"You should know that Kunststoff will use his lobbying network to make problems for Mesopelogic."

"Yes, I know. That's the work we have in front of us."

"Sarah, if there's anything else you find out that might help, will you let me know?" Ember asks.

"I can't be a party to that, but I'll just pretend I didn't hear it," the governor says and smiles.

Sarah hears the door open behind her, turns around, and Kunststoff is just a few inches away.

"What in hell are you doing out here? I was looking everywhere for you," he growls, eyes bulging.

Sarah lowers the phone down by her side.

"I needed some fresh air."

CHAPTER 33

OIKOPLEURA DIOICA
{TRANSPARENT - PELAGIC
TUNICATES - APPENDICULARIA}

Tilly dials a retro telephone in the cottage. Frida, a pretty older woman in her late fifties with long salt and pepper hair and brown eyes, rows a wood canoe on an alpine lake.

"Hello," Friday answers.

"It's Tilly."

"Mi hija. How are you?"

Frida has become a close confidante and spiritual sage to Tilly over the years.

"I'm fine. How are you?"

"I'm on the lake catching a few fish, letting the big Bear sleep in. He's getting old, you know."

"That's loving of you. Any bites?"

"Of course. You know I tie the best flies."

Tilly is silent.

"What is it?"

Frida waits. "Tilly, breathe."

Tilly takes a deep breath. "Yes, thank you. I just had to hear your voice. I don't love technology all the time, but I'm relieved that I reached you out in the middle of the lake. I'm feeling lost."

"Yes?"

Tilly speaks quickly without taking a breath. "I saw Moore and I'm in the middle of this training and its so hard and I'm in an entirely different place than I'm used to and I'm with Liam and it's new and Graham and Camas are quarreling about my training all the time as usual and it's hot and the mountains are big piles of rocks with no trees here and you aren't here." She starts to cry. "Or mom and dad."

They sit in silence and close their eyes.

"I hear you. Can you hear me?" Frida asks.

"Yes."

"When is the race?"

"In one week."

"If I give you my advice, will you take it?"

"Yes."

"Tell Liam, Camas, and Graeme that you love them. Thank them very much and then tell them that you need to go away for a few days and that you will see them no later than the morning of the day before the race."

"They won't understand."

"Perhaps."

"What will I do when I go away?"

"You will figure that out."

"I miss you. Thank you, Frida."

"Peace, dear one."

Moore draws in his sketchbook, sitting at the galley table. He answers his phone.

"Tilly. What's up?"

"Would you like to go to the Pu'u Loa Petroglyphs with

me? It would be a camping overnight. I hear the petroglyphs are pretty cool. P's been bugging me to find you ever since you two met."

Moore laughs. "Sure. When and where?"

"I have two more days of intense training, so Wednesday?"

"I'll have to find a babysitter for Spit."

"I'll ask Liam and the guys to look after him. Keep him out of trouble."

"Not sure that's possible. Where should we meet, and what do I need?"

"Bring hiking boots and swim trunks. Can you come to our cottage? It's at the end of Leilani Hill Road."

"Cool."

CHAPTER 34
DOLIOLUM DENTICULATUM
{TRANSPARENT - PELAGIC
TUNICATES - DOLIOLIDA}

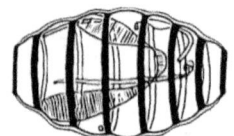

Camas busts into Tilly's cottage.

"Hey there," Tilly says. "What have you been up to besides kissing Josh?"

"Taking care of your business. Someone's got to."

"Where is Josh?"

"Surfing with the guys." She smiles dreamily. "Damn, my guy is sexy." She turns serious. "Don't distract me. I've found the perfect sponsor for you."

"You know I don't like sponsors."

"This sport is expensive, and I think this one could help your causes."

"Who is it?"

"I have a Facetime set up in five."

"Gee, thanks for the heads up."

"I didn't want you to say no."

"I can say no now," Tilly says defiantly.

"Really?" Camas says with a whine, worried.

"Call them for goodness sake."

Camas sets her Macbook on the coffee table and calls Ember. Ember appears on the screen.

"Hi, Camas. How are you?" Ember says energetically.

"Ember, this is Tilly."

"So nice to meet you, Tilly. I'm a big fan of your One More Year project."

"Thanks. Nice to meet you too."

"Ember is the CEO and founder of WowFlo. They've been a big contributor to the OMY billboards."

"Thank you so much," Tilly says gratefully.

"We'd like to sponsor your Ironman competition."

"I'm pretty far into it. Not too much left to sponsor. As you've probably heard, I don't have outside sponsors."

"We know that. Camas thought you might listen to our proposal."

"I'll listen," Tilly smiles.

"The proposal includes making another donation to One More Year for 50 more billboards, including 20 international cities. Also, we're working on a project we're very proud of – to rid the planet of plastic bottles."

"That seems overwhelming."

"Yes, it's huge. We have the prototype for the first phase of refillable bottles and would like to formally announce the project to the world at the Ironman when you win it."

"I can't guarantee I'll win."

"We know that."

"I'll review the proposal with Camas. I'll consider it."

"Thank you."

Camas touches the screen to end the call. She looks at Tilly, waiting. "Well? We could really use that money for the billboards."

"I'll think about it."

"What's the hesitation."

"I want to make sure they're on the up and up. Just because you can speak green doesn't always mean your blood is green."

"True that."

"You do some digging too, sista."

"You got it."

Spit pulls into Tilly's driveway in Ike's woodie wagon. He and Moore get out of the car and pet Pedro as Tilly walks out of the cottage. Liam carries out her backpack and tosses it into the rear of their Jeep rental. Pedro jumps into the back of the jeep.

"Cool wagon," Liam says.

"Ike let me borrow it," Spit says.

"Turns out we don't need tents. There's a place we can stay."

"Great," Moore answers.

Liam kisses Tilly.

"Have fun, you two."

Spit tries to kiss Moore. "Yeah, go have some ohana fun."

Moore pushes Spit away, laughing, then hugs him.

"Don't go wild when I'm gone."

"I'll try."

"We're going to a live music show at the beach tonight," Liam says.

"Uh oh. Use the buddy system," Moore warns.

Tilly and Moore hop into the jeep with Pedro and wave as they drive off. Pedro barks.

CHAPTER 35
NEMATOSCELIS DIFFICILIS {CRUSTACEANS - EUPHAUSIIDS - EUPHAUSIACEA}

"We got Tilly DeMontagne!" Ember says with her arms triumphantly raised to the sky.

Ember walks through the WowFlo production facility with her head engineer, Raul, who wears a white lab coat with the WowFlo logo. Raul hands her a sleek blue aluminum bottle and points to the refill station. Ember places it on a circular marker, and the machine fills the bottle to the top, no spills.

"Looks ready!"

"We're just making some adjustments, so it's more flexible with different bottle sizes."

"How long until we're in production?"

"30 to 45 days."

"I like one number."

"45 then."

Ember smiles warmly. "Make it 20, please."

She slaps him on the back. "Nice work!"

Raul starts to respond, "I'm not sure..."

Ember interrupts. "I also need a prototype, a display wagon, and 10,000 refillable branded bottles shipped to the

King Kamehemeha's Kona Beach Hotel by Wednesday before the Ironman race.

"We have a prototype, but not the bottles."

"Make that 20 prototypes so we can fill people's bottles efficiently."

"But..."

"And they need to be branded and say, *Refill, Bill!* with a pug in a superhero cape.

"That's a lot of bottles."

"That's not even a fraction of every person on earth who'll have one."

Raul sighs.

"We've come this far," Ember adds, looking him in the eye.

"We'll make it happen."

"Thank you. I know you can," Ember says confidently.

Ember walks away, then turns back around. "I want you and your Refill Team to be there too. And bring your families."

CHAPTER 36

EMERITA ANALOGA
{CRUSTACEANS - DECAPODS - DECAPODA}

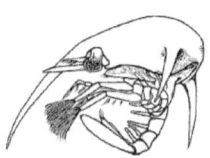

T illy and Moore drive the Jeep along the coast to a volcano and then to the ancient petroglyphs at Pu'uLoa where they see sea turtles etched on ancient cave walls. Pedro barks at sea turtles on the beach. They drive back down to the coast into a small fishing village with a harbor and boat dock with colorful fishing boats and a handful of sailboats. They park and walk with Pedro and their backpacks to the boat dock.

Tilly looks at her phone, then points to a sailboat.

"I think this is our boat for the night."

"Terrific. How do we eat?" Moore asks.

"They told me there's a small restaurant on the beach."

"I think I see it over there. It's only three o'clock. Let's take the boat out. I bet that restaurant would cook a fish if we catch one."

"I don't know how to sail."

"I'll teach you. It's not too windy but windy enough to have a little sail. The boat looks yar. Game?"

"Sure."

"Great."

They get into the boat with their packs, and Pedro jumps in after them. Moore unties the boat from the dock. He points to the rope on the mainsail.

"Untie that sheet."

"What sheet?"

"A sheet is a rope. That one there. Just unwrap it, and I'll tell you what to do next."

"Why don't they just call it a rope?" Tilly says under her breath.

"I heard that." Moore smiles. "There are a lot of sailing terms that are hundreds of years old, like halyard. That's the rope that pulls the sail up."

"Who knew?"

"You didn't ask about 'yar.'"

"Camas and Sarah Jessica Parker taught me that word. How did you get into sailing?"

Moore pets Pedro. "When Mom and Dad died, and I moved to L.A., I wanted to get off of land. I was riding my bike along the water and saw a marina. I walked my bike around it, looking at the boats, when a couple of guys asked me if I wanted to go out with them. It hooked me. I took some classes and hung out by that marina and crewed whenever I could."

"That's so cool."

"I dragged Spit into it. He was reluctant and still complains, but I think he actually likes it."

The wind fills the sail.

"Take the helm and point us towards that big cloud on the horizon."

"Got it."

Moore trims the sail and raises the jib. Pedro barks in excitement. Moore looks back and smiles at them both.

CHAPTER 37

MERTENSIA OVUM
{TRANSPARENT - CTENOPHORES
- CYDIPPIDA}

Josh and Camas dance barefoot in the sand in front of a beachside bar. The Bike Guys each dance with partners, and Liam and Spit sit at a high table with beers in front of them. Pedro relaxes on the sand below, watching the dancers.

"Why don't you ask a girl to dance?" Liam asks Spit.

"I don't see any. Why do Josh and the guys have to be so buff?"

"You're pretty buff."

Spit looks down to his arms. "Bullshit, but thanks, man."

"Hey, you're a sailor, and you have P as your wingman."

Camas overhears. "Spit, come dance with me."

"OK with you, Josh?"

"Sure."

Spit dances very dramatically and comically. Camas plays along, laughing. Pedro is jumping and dancing with them on the edge of the dance floor. Spit makes a twirling move and bumps into Anika.

"Hey, watch it," Anika says sternly.

Spit is lovestruck. He is tall but still has to look up to Anika.

"I'm so sorry. You're beautiful."

Anika has a skeptical look on her face.

"Aren't you Anika Jambes?" Camas asks.

"Yes."

"Good luck next week."

"Thanks."

Spit turns to Camas and speaks in a hushed voice. "You know her?"

"She's a major Ironman triathlete, ding dong."

"She's a goddess."

"I think she likes your dancing. She's imitating you."

"Really?"

Spit looks over, and Anika is laughing with her friends, looking back over at Spit and dancing wildly.

"Go dance with her."

"Are you sure?"

Camas pushes Spit towards Anika. "Grow some balls."

Spit walks over to Anika tentatively but with his chest puffed out, still making his silly dance moves as he approaches.

"Anika? I'm Spit. Can I dance with you?"

Anika looks at him dancing, letting a little smile crack her serious face.

"Are you going to keep dancing all lolo like that?" she asks seriously.

"Lolo?"

"Goofy."

"Probably."

"Good."

They continue the dramatic, comical dancing, Anika getting more and more into it as they go.

"Anika, you're a goddess."

"Yeah?"

"Yeah."

"Anika Jambes?"

"Yes?"

"You're my jam."

Anika smiles and leans down to kiss Spit on the lips.

CHAPTER 38

CAVOLINIA INFLEXA {SHELLS - PTEROPODS - THECOSOMATA}

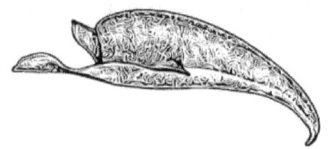

Moore sits on the side of the sailboat as Tilly holds the wheel.

"Steer toward that point."

"This is fun!"

"Even though you're not powering the speed yourself?"

"Especially so. What a nice break! Where are we going?"

"I think Kumilo Beach is this way. I want to show you something."

They approach a rocky point, and Moore takes the helm.

"Till, I'm going to say 'prepare to come about.' The sail is going to swing to the other side. Make sure you duck, OK? When the sail is on the other side, I'll ask you to trim the sail by tightening the sheet."

"OK."

"Ready?"

"Ready!"

Moore turns the boat. "Prepare to come about!"

The sail comes quickly across the sailboat.

"Now trim the sail until you don't see any fluttering."

"How's that?"

"Great!"

"That was exciting!"

They come around the point to see a large sandy beach. Their faces drop.

"What in goddess's name..." her voice trails off.

"It's plastic trash."

"What?"

"I've only read about Kamilo Beach. It's called the dirtiest beach in the world. Trade winds push the plastic in currents, and they say this area is like a sieve."

As they get closer, they see a person walking along the beach, picking things up.

"Can we go to shore?"

"Sure. There's a dinghy."

Moore takes down the sail, throws out the anchor. They get into the dinghy, and Pedro tries to jump in.

"P, no. Stay."

Pedro whimpers at the edge of the sailboat. Moore rows toward shore. Pedro jumps out of the sailboat and swims after them. Tilly shakes her head and laughs. They keep a close eye on him as they motor to shore.

A large older Hawaiian man walks towards them with a broad smile. "Aloha. How are you?"

"We're doing really well. I just learned to sail," Tilly says proudly.

"How did she do?"

"She's a natural."

"This beach is so sad. All of this plastic." Tilly looks around.

"Yes. What's even sadder is when a dolphin, seal, turtle, or whale wash up either caught in plastic or filled up with plastic or both," the man says solemnly.

"Oh, no."

"I'm afraid so."

He holds out his hand, "My name is Holokai. You can call me Holo."

"I'm Moore." Moore shakes Holo's hand. "This is Tilly. And P."

Tilly shakes Holo's hand as he pets Pedro.

"What are you picking up? There's so much trash for one person."

Holo turns around and starts walking away down the beach. "Come."

Moore and Tilly look at each other and follow. Pedro trots along behind, sniffing the plastic objects. Holo leads them to an area of the beach with huge sculptures of whales, dolphins, and fish made out of plastic water containers, soda containers, plastic rings, straws, plastic bags, and other mystery plastic pieces. The sculptures also contain bones.

"Are those bones?" Tilly asks, surprised.

"Yes."

"Can I take some photos?" Moore asks.

"That would be fine."

Moore wanders off.

"How long have you been making art out here?" Tilly asks.

"About three years. I've been coming here my whole life and trying to pick up the plastic that's gotten worse and worse over my lifetime. I was at the point of deep despair, and one day, a large whale washed up with her dead baby and plastic inside. That day, in mourning, I just started stacking things, and then the next day, I brought some wire and glue. The first sculpture," Holo says, pointing, "was the whale over there."

"I think your sculptures should be shown around the world, Holo."

"Probably so," he says gently.

Moore walks up, snapping a few more photos. "We should probably get back to the harbor."

"It's been nice meeting you. Good luck at the race, Tilly."

Tilly is surprised, "How did you know?"

"That's a good question. I'm usually out here on my own, mostly. I go into town for groceries. I keep a canoe at Waipouli Lake where I grew up because sometimes feel I need to be on gentler water."

"I know the feeling," Tilly says longingly.

"I went to town and saw a newspaper with your photo. I bought some food and took it out to my canoe on the lake. I don't know what to say, but I felt like I knew you already."

Holo reaches into his shorts pocket. "I made this for you."

He pulls out his closed fist and rests it gently on top of Tilly's open hand. He pauses, closes his eyes as if in prayer, and opens his hand. Tilly looks at Moore, eyes wide, then carefully at the bracelet. It has small sea creatures carved out of shells, bone, and plastic.

"It's beautiful. I don't know what to say," she says, a tear in her eye.

"Just say that you'll continue to always feel for this earth."

Moore puts the bracelet on Tilly's wrist.

"I will!" Tilly says as she hugs Holo strongly.

CHAPTER 39

CRESEUS VIRGULA {SHELLS - PTEROPODS - THECOSOMATA}

Kunststoff is on a golf course on the coast and hits a shot towards the ocean onto the green.

"Yes!" he says with an awkward twirl.

His private caddy answers his cell phone.

"It's Sarah, sir."

"Tell her I'll call her when I'm off the course," he says, annoyed.

The caddy hands over the phone. "She says it's urgent."

Kunststoff shakes his head, frustrated. He listens. "Yes, of course, I know the board meeting's tomorrow!"

Moore walks down the dock to his sailboat. Spit and Anika are listening to ABBA, playing chess, and drinking beer.

Hey buddy. Welcome back! Anika, this is Moore.

"Hello," she says seriously.

"Nice to meet you."

Moore turns his head toward Spit, so Anika can't see. With raised eyebrows, he silently mouths, "What?"

"How was the trip?" Spit asks, smiling.

"Interesting."

Anika stands up, kisses Spit. "Gotta train."

"Don't leave," Spit says with a sad puppy face.

Anika kisses him on the cheek. "I'll see you, my lolo."

"Don't be a stranger!" he calls as she runs down the dock.

"Wow. Who was that?!"

"A triathlete goddess."

"She's twice your size."

"Yup," Spit says dreamily.

"I think she's Tilly's main competition."

"I don't doubt it."

Moore takes out his phone to show Spit photos from Kamilo Beach. "Check these out."

"Those are amazing and scary at the same time."

"We found them out on Kamilo Beach, along with mounds and mounds of plastic coming from the currents."

"It sucks that the beach is doing a better job than the scoop up machine."

Sarah types quickly on an iMac at her kitchen table in her tiny studio apartment. A town cruiser bike hangs on the wall, and photos of Zak Effron, Tilly DeMontagne, and Sylvia Earle are on the frig. Her calico cat, Lucy, purrs on her lap as she drinks peppermint tea and references a large stack of files.

"Where in goddess's name have you been?" Camas asks, sitting on the beach next to Josh on her phone.

"I told you. I took a couple of days off."

"I told Ember you said yes. She was very excited."

"Thank you. I'm happy you're taking some time off too."

Camas kisses Josh. "Yeah, it's so amazing here. Let's stay," she jokes. "Ember wanted to make sure we knew something."

"What's that?"

"She said she's not exactly sure how best to make the announcement. She'll have the refill prototype and free bottles for the crowd. But, with the short notice, she's not sure how to give it the launch it deserves."

"That was honest." Tilly is silent, thinking. "I have an idea. We may have some people who can help with that."

"You can tell me, your CFO-in-saving-the-world, when I bring over your WowFlo triathlon kit."

CHAPTER 40

PYROSOMA ATLANTICUM
{TRANSPARENT - PELAGIC
TUNICATES - PYROSOMIDA}

Kunststoff, Sarah, and ten board members sit around a large conference table. Kunststoff is looking through the papers in front of him. "Sarah, do you the report?" he says gruffly.

"Yes, sir."

Sarah passes the report to Kunststoff and walks around the table, placing the papers in front of each member.

"Thank you," he says.

Sarah rolls her eyes in the other direction at his fake politeness.

Kunststoff reads from the report, "The scoop up project started on track, and although it had some early difficulties, and those difficulties were initially thought to be solvable, we now find that there may be insurmountable prob..."

He stops abruptly, his face turning red in a fury. "What is this?!"

He sees the others have started reading.

"Wait, gentlemen, ladies..."

Kunststoff tries to retrieve the report from the others, but they've already begun reading. A female board member,

Ms. Whitacre, wearing a navy dress and pearls, holds tight onto her report when Kunststoff tries to take it.

Mr. White, a tall, handsome man in his late sixties with short gray hair, speaks up. "Sarah, why don't you fill us in on your report, please."

Sarah glares defiantly at Kunststoff. "Yes, Mr. White. The scoop up machine is harming wildlife, and it's not capturing plastic as intended. The report in your hands includes information on a new bill written by Senator Mesopelogic of Oregon that will require SodaCo and other beverage companies and plastic producers to change their manufacturing to a 100% refillable model. As you may recall, we started research on this and had some promising results."

"What's the status of that project?" Ms. Whitacre asks.

"It's stall..."

Kunststoff cuts Saraha off. "It's in development."

"WowFlo has a *completed* prototype."

"If we'll have penalties from the government and are behind the eightball, we need to get that project rolling," Mr. White says.

The other board members nod in agreement.

Kunststoff is silent, fuming.

"Do you agree?" Ms. Whitacre asks pointedly.

Kunststoff mumbles unintelligible angry words under his breath.

"If you aren't behind this project, maybe we need to find a CEO who will be," Mr. White says sternly.

"I'm behind it, God damn it!" he shouts, eyes attempting to launch darts to pierce Sarah's pure heart.

CHAPTER 41

CYCLOSALPA BAKERI
{TRANSPARENT - PELAGIC
TUNICATES - SALPIDA}

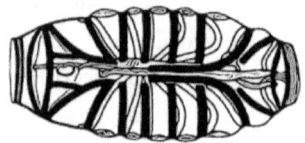

"Holo, I need your help," Tilly says, getting an athletic massage from Liam on a table on the beach in front of the cottage.

"What is it?"

"Can we borrow ten of your biggest sculptures?"

"Of course."

"I don't know how we'll move them."

"I do."

"I also need some big guys to help us on the day of the race. Can I send some of our friends over to see you and help make a good plan?"

"Your friends are my friends."

"One small detail. It's for race day, day after tomorrow."

"A'ole pilikia. No problem."

"Mahalo, Holo."

Tilly and Moore stand on the marina dock, his boat in the background.

"I need your help."

"You look nervous. Race nerves?"

"No, not that. Well, sort of. We need a video that can help convince people to get rid of their plastic disposables for good."

"That's a tall order."

"I know. But I think we have the components. WowFlo has a prototype of their beverage refill station, and they're ready to launch it at the race. We just need something powerful to go with it. Can you and Spit work on that?"

"On it. Send over the WowFlo thing."

"I will. One more thing. Well, two more."

"What's that?"

"It can't be boring."

"Not a snoozer. Got it. And?"

"It needs to be done by the end of the race. Let Camas know when you have it and send it to her."

"Done."

"Mahalo, brother."

"I have something for you," Moore says, handing her a tiny wrapped package.

Tilly opens it.

"It's a kolea!"

"I thought you could add it to your Holo bracelet. The kolea are aumakua, protector spirits. I want you to have a safe race."

"No," Tilly shakes her head.

"No?" Moore looks hurt.

"It needs to be on my locket necklace," she says, taking it off her neck and stringing on the charm.

Moore smiles. She turns around, and he clasps the chain.

CHAPTER 42

HOLMESIMYSIS COSTATA {CRUSTACEANS - MYSIDS - MYSIDACEA}

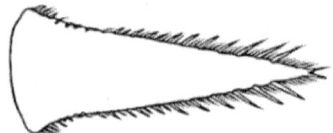

Huge boxes with WowFlo logos are unloaded off of a Fedex cargo plane. Raul, the WowFlo engineering team, and their families get leis as they exit the aircraft at the Kona airport. Raul answers his cell phone.

"Aloha! Welcome to Hawaii!" Ember says excitedly.

Colorful, mystical, magical images of the tiniest of fish and plankton, sparkling and swimming around, are intermixed with plastic pieces on a large computer screen in front of Spit. Moore, Hop, and Zara stand behind him, peering at the fascinating images. Hop and Zara's island house on the coast is similar to their boat, classy, French-inspired, containing a lab area with microscopes and computers.

"It's a fish phantasmagoria. Thank god I didn't smoke before this."

"Yes, thank goodness," Zara agrees.

"This is just the one bucket you scooped and look at all of

those creatures! It's like the image we saw on your boat but with plastic too. What's in there exactly?" Moore asks.

"I know a couple of guys studying this. They didn't intend to study plastic, but there was so much of it in the larval fish, they had to. They were amazed that the surface contains such a diverse group of fish. They found deep-sea fish, mid-ocean fish, and reef fish all interacting at the surface for the first few weeks of their lives. It was so unique. Can you think of any other place on earth where babies from different areas share nursery grounds?"

"The concern is that the plastic the baby fish are eating is making the already difficult early survival days harder and that the fish populations will continue to diminish."

"Then add to their troubles a machine scooping up the neuston!" Moore adds.

"What's the neuston again?" Spit asks.

"The baby fish and plankton, ding dong," Moore answers.

"Oh, yeah."

"Ganja short term memory loss?"

"Probs," Spit says, considering the possibility. He looks back at the screen. "These will work well, and it's got to have music," Spit says.

"You pick that," Moore responds.

"And I think it needs some extra fun in there somewhere," Spit adds.

"Let's get the main task done, and then we'll see if we can work in fun," Hop suggests.

"How are we going to get onto that jumbotron?" Moore asks.

"I think I've got a race contact that can help us. She owes me a favor."

"We know the scoop up machine has problems, but what if the guy that made the machine is trying to do the right thing?" Moore asks.

"Don't get all soft on us now," Spit says.

"You're a good man, Moore. However, his entire business model is based on selling plastic to pay for the operation. He doesn't have much incentive to solve the core issue."

"The machine is like trying to clean up blood on the floor in an emergency room when the patient is still bleeding," Zara says kindly.

"You're right."

"Anika knows the dude, man. Las Periteur is Belgian. She's Belgian. He contacted her about sponsorship."

"Can she call him? Maybe he'll join our cause."

"Can't hurt," Zara says.

"I'll ask her. Now, what other components do we have?" Spit asks.

"We also have the WowFlo and Holo stuff," Moore reminds him.

"Young Spit, I didn't know you could edit," Hop says.

"I make art films and music videos at school, but yeah, I know my way around a bit."

"It's all yours then. You're the man for the job. Do you need anything else?"

"Didn't I see a turntable?"

"Yes. I'll get it."

"Awesome. That's it. I'll let you know when I have the first cut."

Spit puts his headphones on and gets to work on the computer.

Zara brings him the turntable and some albums in French. Hop brings him a plate of food. Moore brings him a beer. Esme brings him a kiss.

Camas walks along Kamilo beach. She looks carefully at Holo's plastic sculptures and is struck by the sad significance. She wells up in tears as Ike and The Bike Guys walk up.

"How in the hell will we get these to the finish?" Camas says, quickly wiping her eyes.

"I have a farming friend nearby with some trucks," Holo suggests.

"Can you see if he can help?" Ike asks.

Holo makes a quick call.

"We also need about twenty strong men or women and forty wheels for the pallets when we get to town," Josh says.

Holo ends his call. "Hiki nō. No problem. My friend said he will be here in fifteen minutes. I'll make some calls to get some island muscle and the wheels. Just so you're not surprised when the trucks arrive, my friend farms pakalolo."

"We're fans of the pakalolo," Camas says.

The Bike Guys laugh and nod.

"It will be tight timing to get to the podium, but I think we can do it. Holo, we'll need you to be with the helpers, and we'll spread out along the route and let you the best path. Keep your phone close," Camas says.

They all work to move the sculptures and pallets near the road. They are struggling with the size and weight.

"What if we get these all the way over there, and she doesn't win?" Cutter asks, sweating.

"Don't speak those words," Camas says firmly.

Two large trucks arrive. The friendly Hawaiian farmers exit the trucks and give Holo and the others a handshake and a hug. They open the back of the truck, and the smell wafts out. The group leans in in unison to take a large inhale. They close their eyes and smile.

CHAPTER 43
THALIA DEMOCRATICA
{TRANSPARENT - PELAGIC
TUNICATES - SALPIDA}

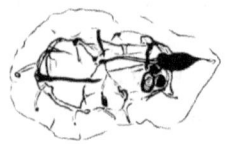

The heroes move through the last few days before the Ironman in a race of speed, a race for justice, and a race for an opala- (oh-pa-la) free moana (mow-AH-nah).

Senator Mesopelogic sits with other members of Congress debating the refill bill in committee.

Kunststoff digs through the office files looking for the Refill Project report. He gives up in frustration and walks out of his office. Sarah walks out of the SodaCo building with a box of her personal office belongings.

Moore and Spit sit together in front of the computer talking seriously, then laughing and singing. They each alternate putting a casual arm over the back of the chair around their best sailing friend and point to the screen as they edit the film. They stand and dance in hip hop style.

Festivities before the race begin at the Ironman Parade of Nations event at the Marriott King Kamehameha Kona Beach Hotel. Hundreds of athletes and spectators mingle to upbeat music. Camas and Tilly dance in the crowd.

Camas, Josh, and Sarah sit at a computer reviewing an image of a new billboard for Refill, Bill! They point to the graphic, discussing changes.

Tilly sleeps next to Liam with Pedro at the foot of their bed the night before the race. The alarm goes off at 3:00 am.

Senator Mesopelogic is at the White House meetings with groups of one or two people, building support for the bill. Reactions vary from positive to skeptical to anger. A few shake his hand.

Kunststoff is in a rage, throwing and kicking things in his office. An office assistant walks the Refill Report a few feet from his desk to where he stands in a tirade.

Camas is on the phone with Moore and Spit working on the video as she balances on a surfboard in her living room.

Tilly is in a swarm of triathletes getting numbers drawn in Sharpie on their shoulders. They jump up and down and stretch as they wait to enter the water to start the Ironman. The huge crowd cheers as helicopters with cameras fly over.

Ember is in a large hotel meeting room filled with WowPom boxes. She takes a water bottle out of one of the boxes and puts it onto the refill station prototype. It fills with crystal clear water. She drinks it all, closing her eyes peacefully. She squats down and shows the superhero pug graphic on the bottle to Plastic.

Tilly swims in a large group of Ironman swimmers and begins pulling away.

Raul's wife is on the beach with their five-year-old daughter. She holds a Dory fish and sings sweetly, "Just keep swimming, swimming, swimming..."

Senator Mesopelogic is at the podium in front of the House of Representatives presenting his bill.

CHAPTER 44

THETYS VAGINA {TRANSPARENT - PELAGIC TUNICATES - SALPIDA}

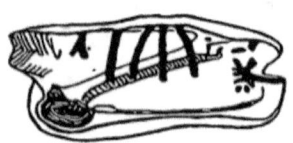

Graeme and Liam stand near the exit of the Ironman swim. Tilly is the first female out, followed by Anika. There is a substantial gap before the other female triathletes begin exiting the water.

"She did it," Graeme says, patting Liam on the back.

"One down, two to go," Liam says nervously.

Tilly runs to the transition area, pulls on her helmet and bike shoes. She jumps on her bike with Anika just behind. Anika passes Tilly in the transition area. The cyclists race out of Kailua-Kona then past dramatic scorching lava fields.

Spit and Moore are just off the coast in Moore's boat. They look at their phones.

"She's in third behind Anika and another rider," Moore says.

Spit whoops, excitedly. "You go, girl!"

"Who are you rooting for?"

"What?" Spit answers innocently.

"You said, 'you go, girl.' Who's the girl?"

"My girlfriend, I guess."

"Dude, you can't root for Anika."

"I can't?"

"No."

Spit whoops just as enthusiastically, "Tilly, whoo hoo! You go, girl!"

"OK, man. Finish up the video! We have to get it to Camas!"

"Almost done! Ready the dinghy, captain!"

The scoop up machine is loaded onto a barge.

"Yes sir, got the message," the captain replies on the phone.

"Who was that?" a crewman asks.

"SodaCo pulled out. They wanted to make sure we are packing up."

CHAPTER 45

DOSIDICUS GIGAS {SQUID - SQUID - TEUTHIDA}

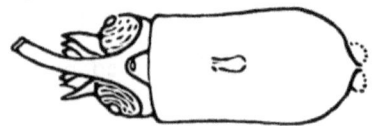

"I've meant to ask how you started WowFlo."

Sarah wears a pretty Hawaiian print dress with a lei around her neck. She and Ember are standing in the quaint downtown area of Hawi, waiting for the Ironman cyclists to come through the small town as they turn around back to Kona.

"I came to Los Angeles to become an actress."

"Wow."

"I was an outstanding waitress."

Sarah laughs.

"My family has a lot of money. My great grandfather bought the rights to distribute the Day Dreamer lily, which became the best selling flower almost everywhere. He kind of scammed the inventor out of any of the riches, and from a very young age, I've always wanted to do something to overcome that bad family karma."

"Like what?"

"I knew I could help people be healthier, so I came up with the WowFlo vita-fruit line. Then, when I saw how much plastic we were putting into the world from the success, we created the refillable machines. I envision someday people being able to have special water that includes the vitamins and minerals their body is missing. We'd have their profile, and when they set their aluminum bottle on the machine, their personalized health drink would come out."

"I'd love that!"

"We'll start with the refillable water and our health drinks first. Then we'll aim for the fountain of youth!" Ember laughs.

They look towards the street. The crowd is bustling with excitement.

"How's Tilly doing?" Sarah asks.

"Excellent! She's in third place behind Anika and Zoe Stewart, the New Zealand contender."

"Any word from Mesopelogic?"

"He's in front of the House as we speak."

"Is the launch ready to go?"

"The prototype's ready. Tilly said she'd be our spokesperson if she wins. It's in her hands."

The spectators lining the streets of the tiny town drink from plastic containers, eat convenience foods in plastic wrappers, and use straws to drink sugar-overloaded beachside tourist drinks. There is plastic trash on the ground amidst the crowd. A young man opens a SodaCo cola and drops the red plastic cap onto the sidewalk behind him as he walks away. Ember shakes her head and squats down to pick it up.

The crowd erupts in cheers as the cyclists enter the town.

"Here they come!" Ember exclaims.

The cyclists, led by Anika, Zoe, then Tilly, race through Hawi as the spectators cheer. Tilly, in her WowFlo kit, perspires from the extreme heat.

CHAPTER 46

LIMACINA HELICINA {SHELLS - PTEROPODS - THECOSOMATA}

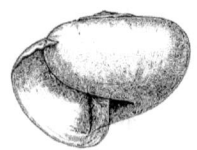

Tilly runs along a stretch of coastline with harsh lava beds on one side and cool, blue ocean on the other. Her breath is labored. Tilly makes her move, picking up her pace to overtake the New Zealand athlete.

Moore and Spit tie up the dinghy in the Kona harbor and run at full speed to find the finish line sound booth. Moore plays the live feed on his phone.

A commentator shouts, "Tilly DeMontagne has overtaken second-place runner Zoe Stewart."

Moore and Spit jump up and do a sumo wrestler belly-bounce with a high five.

"Yes!"

They laugh and continue running.

Tilly finds the strength to keep pace with Anika. She feels Holo's bracelet bouncing on her wrist and knows the entire WowFlo launch rests on her shoulders. She digs deep into her deep love for the planet to increase her speed and reach Anika's long stride. Anika is startled, then angry, as Tilly pulls ahead. Anika stays close behind, their faces in painful grimaces just one mile from the finish.

The Speaker of the House calls a vote. A representative is asleep in his chair.

"As many as are in favor, as the question may be, say, 'Aye.'"

A large group of representatives calls out "Aye!"

"As many as are opposed, say 'No.'"

Ember and Graeme stand in the crowd at Kailua Pier, where the Ironman athletes will soon be finishing.

Ember looks at her phone. "Oh, my god. She's in the lead!"

Ember hugs the first person she sees. He is surprised.

"You're Graeme Selkirk!"

"Yes. Do I know you?"

"No, you don't. I was at the Tour when you had your accident. I'm Ember, and Tilly is representing WowFlo, my company. Don't you coach Tilly?"

Graeme puts his arm around Liam.

"I'm one of her coaches, yes, and this is her swim coach, Liam."

"You've done a great job."

"She's truly a natural, that one. Heart and strength. You're lucky she said yes," Graeme says, straining to try to see Tilly approaching.

"I know." Ember sees the racers. "Here they come!"

Liam turns to Graeme, "She's struggling."

Anika is close behind Tilly in the last grueling paces of the race. They look strong as they break through body-breaking exhaustion. Crowds are thick on either side of the road, cheering loudly as they come down Ali'i Drive, nearing the finish line.

The crowd shouts, "Tilly! Tilly! Tilly!" including a heavy set Hawaiian local with his hat on backward.

"Why are you rooting for Tilly?" Sarah asks.

"For starters, she's not haole. And, she's hoaloha with Holo."

Sarah is confused by the answer. She nods her head in island appreciation. "Go, Tilly!"

CHAPTER 47

SARDINOPS SAGAX CAERULEUS {OTHERS - FISH EGGS AND LARVAE}

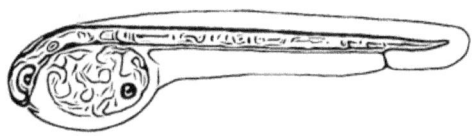

Camas stands with Graeme and Liam in the crowd near the finish line. She texts Holo. *Tilly's in the lead almost to the finish. Standby to move in.* Then to Moore. *Where's the video?!*

"She's still in the lead," Liam says seriously.

"That's my girl," Camas and Graeme say in unison.

Tilly runs fiercely, her legs having to make more strides to compensate for her shorter stature. She appears almost delicate with Anika looming just behind her. Tilly holds her own with Anika at her heels.

"Here they come!" the commentator shouts.

Ember walks against the hoards of people like a fish upstream with Plastic in her arms. The crowd cheers loudly around her. She answers her cell phone, morosely.

"We got the House. Now we take it to the Senate," Senator Mesopelogic says matter of factly.

"Good work."

"How'd she do?"

Ember pauses.

"She didn't win."

"Oh," he says, disappointed.

"We need to plan another launch," she says as she makes her way through the crowds.

Moore and Spit weave quickly through the crowd and spot Hop and Zara at the sound booth. Spit hands the flash drive to Hop who speaks with a woman in the booth. Moore texts Camas. *At the soundbooth! Hop's got the video.*

"Sorry, dude, I swear I was rooting for Tilly."

"That's OK, buddy. If we felt trying our hardest always has to mean winning, we would never try anything."

"Wow, that's so philosophical."

They are silent as they walk through the crowds towards the winner's podium.

"I hope she's OK.""She is."

"Bummer that we won't need the video."

CHAPTER 48
MITROCOMA DISCOIDEA {TRANSPARENT - JELLYFISH - HYDROZOA: LEPTOTHECATAE}

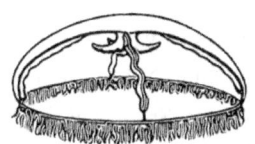

The winning triathletes are on the podium, Anika in the center, Tilly on the right, Zoe on the left. As the crowd cheers, the mayor of Kailua-Kona puts the third-place medal around Zoe's neck, then the second-place medal around Tilly's. Tilly bows her head in a reserved acceptance.

The crowds' cheers increase. The mayor puts the first place medal around Anika's neck. More wild applause. He hands the mic to Anika.

The crowd quiets, waiting for Anika to speak. TV cameras are filming. Anika looks around at the spectators in all directions without speaking.

The mayor whispers in her ear, "Anika, dear, would you like to address the crowd?"

Anika remains quiet.

Camas calls Holo with instructions. His group of strong Hawaiian helpers, along with Ike and The Bike guys, are in traditional island dress and they roll Holo's sculptures down Kaluia town streets toward the race.

"That's OK if you prefer not to say anyth..."

Anika interrupts the mayor, speaking loudly into the mic, "Yes, I would."

She looks around and stalls.

"This is my friend Tilly DeMontagne," she says.

Ember stops abruptly. She turns around to listen from a distance. The crowd cheers loudly.

Anika pulls Tilly and Zoe up onto the top podium level with her.

"And this is my other good friend, Zoe Stewart."

The crowd cheers louder.

Anika finally hears the sound of Hawaiian drums in the distance.

She calls out at the top of her voice, "We'd like to show you something!"

The Hawaiian drumming gets louder and louder. Male and female dancers sway and move to island music as they make their way up the runners' path towards the winners' podium.

The mayor is startled by the music. "What is this?"

He sees the dancers. "How wonderful! Everyone, we get another show!"

The crowd cheers as they move to the music.

Suddenly, there are gasps from the crowd as Holo's large plastic and bone sculptures make their way through the finishing line towards the podium, pushed by Holo's and Tilly's friends.

The music continues, and the men and women push the sculptures around the perimeter of the podium, then begin to dance for the crowd. Two men in costume part of the official awards on either side of the winner's podium, dance along with them. Ike and The Bike Guys dance enthusiastically. As the dancing ends, the drummers continue pounding very powerfully and then stop abruptly.

"We have something important to show you. Fais attention!" Annika calls out.

The drumming begins again loudly and blends into the same beat in the video on the giant jumbotron screen above the winners' podium. A large image of earth from space appears with the areas of the planet's plastic garbage patches clearly seen.

The drummers stop, and the beat in the video continues loudly. The crowd quiets.

Moore and Spit appear on the screen. They rap in unison, moving and dancing with hip hop skill. They beat box in expert rhythm after each phrase. Images on the large screen match their words.

Tilly running on Kamilo Beach.

"We're drowning in plastic, up to our ears."

SodaCo plastic bottles coming off the assembly line, branded trash cans overflow with plastic trash.

"Half's been manufactured in just the past fifteen years."

Colorful plankton images fade into a dead whale's open stomach full of plastic.

"Baby fishies think it's food; their moms drown ingestin' it."

Iz with a ukulele dancing on a blanket of plastic in the ocean.

"Great patch is so thick, Iz Kamakawiwo'ole can dance on it."

People drinking out of plastic bottles, buying a plastic container drink.

"You may say but plastic's easy, drop a bill, take a drink."

Smog plumes coming from a plastic manufacturing plant, a mountain of sugar next to a SocaCo cola.

"But plastic kills the planet, air, sea, sugar to the brink."

Tilly runs along the beautiful Hawaiian coastline in the video.

"Tilly ran fast, but someone flew faster."

On stage, Tilly puts her arm around Anika and smiles. In the crowd, Hop and Zara bob their heads to the rap beat. They see Moore and Spit dancing in the crowd and give them a thumbs up.

Plastic the pug running down the beach in a cape, he picks a plastic container up in his mouth.

"He's a pug with a mission, cape hero ever after."

Tilly holds Plastic at a refilling machine and helps him fill up an aluminum bottle.

"Bill's his name and refillin's his game."

Tiny Plastic in his cape sits in front of a wall of plastic at a dumpsite.

"He's here to make a difference, not for fortune or fame."

A rocket ship in the shape of the aluminum refill bottle launches into the sky.

"Bill wants your plastic, to blast it away."

Image of the shiny blue refillable bottle with the pug in a cape graphic.

"And to give you this shiny blue beacon, to refill today."

Tilly, Anika, Zoe, Holo's helpers, the Bike Guys, and Ember's team pass aluminum bottles to the crowd.

The crowd is cheering and excitedly look at their shiny new bottles.

The music turns to a softer beat. Scoop up machine founder, Las Periteur, runs up onto the winner's podium with between Anika and Tilly. Spit and Moore stand behind a cut out of him in the video and continue dancing and bobbing their heads to the beat.

"Hello friends, my name is Las Pirateur, and I invented the plastic scoop up machine. You may have heard of it. We've put the machine on hold because we realized that the problem of plastic is so large, that it would be like standing in your front yard digging a hole to plant a tree for climate change as the dangerous hurricane wind storm swept through your city. The measures we need now are real. Not bandaids."

The crowd cheers loudly.

"I can't tackle this huge problem by myself, and I need your help. WowFlo has an amazing offer for you. Use the free bottle they're passing out today for one year, and they'll pay you $100. Isn't that great! It's so easy. Get your bottle here today and fill it up at one of the refill stations. Use it today, use it tomorrow, use it forever! No more plastic!"

Spit and Moore appear front and center on the screen again, and continue rapping.

"So treat this metal bottle, like a cool gadget for your life."

Images of happy, healthy, hip people of every age and color drinking out of the refillable bottles.

"Don't leave home without it; remind your sister, pops and wife."

Moore and Spit stand in front of a large cardboard box version of the refill station.

"We thank Refill Bill, for flying to save us right here."

The box has a rough hand-drawn label at the top reading 'Corona' and Spit pretends to fill his WowFlo bottle with beer.

"Who knows, one day, it might even give us beer!"

The crowd laughs and cheers.

Ember walks along the waterfront, watching the video on the Ironman livestream. She laughs at the beer image.

"Who knows. Cheers!"

Anika hands the mic to Tilly.

"Thank you, Las. Congratulations, Anika! One more thing, everybody."

The crowd quiets.

"Besides using your awesome new refillable bottle, we need you to call and email your congressman to vote yes on a bill to make all beverage bottles refillable. Go to RefillBil-l.com or WowFlo for their phone numbers. They're scrolling on the video for you now too. Will you do that?"

"Yes!" The crowd cheers.

People are passing water bottles back to others behind them and making calls on their cell phones to their congress-men. The WowFlo team scrambles to get all of the bottles out. The Hawaiian musicians continue playing. Tilly waves to the crowd, hugs Anika and Zoe, then runs off the stage to Liam. They hug and have a sweet kiss. Spectators and triath-letes shake hands with Moore and Spit.

CHAPTER 49
DORYTEUTHIS (LOLIGO) OPALESCENS {SQUID - SQUID - TEUTHIDA}

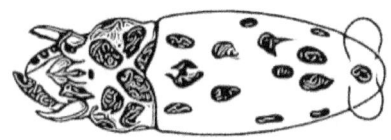

Ember rides her bike along the Venice Beach bike trail with Plastic on the back in his cape. She stops at a stoplight and answers her phone.

"The President signed the bill!" Sarah says.

"Thanks for the call! You know I wanted to hire you, but you got snatched up by the Senator. Congratulations all around!"

Ember laughs and rides on. A *Refill, Bill!* billboard with Plastic in his cape is above her.

Moore, Anika, Hop, Zara, Camas, and Josh play cards on the table on the deck of the Ginette Neveu.

Spit has Esme on his lap and looks out to sea. "What's that?" Spit asks, pointing.

"I think it's my mermaid of a sister."

Tilly climbs out of the water into Moore's boat. Liam and Pedro get out of the kayak. They greet each other with hugs kisses. Pedro is excited to see Esme and barks in excitement. Tilly pulls a skirt and blouse on over her suit.

"I'll get food for you all," Zara says.

"I'll help." Spit follows Zara into the galley.

Moore and Tilly walk to the bow of the boat and look out to sea.

"This is a bit different than Lake Bijou Nez, huh?"

"Yes and no."

"How no?"

"Because I'm here with you."

They are quiet.

"Nice work, iron sister."

"Thanks. You too." Tilly smiles.

"I want to ask you something."

"Sure."

"I was wondering if I can take P across the Atlantic to Europe next summer on the boat."

"Wow."

"Spit, Anika and I would go through the Panama Canal and then over to the Azores, then to Portugal. I know it's a huge question. I understand if you can't be without him. He's such a cool dog."

"Yes, he is." She considers for a moment. "He would love it! Water's in his blood, and maybe he'll learn Portuguese."

Moore laughs and hugs Tilly. "Thank you, Till!"

"He might even help you."

"P, fetch the kayak!" Tilly calls out, gesturing with her arm.

Pedro leaps off the boat, retrieves the rope of the kayak in his mouth, and drags it to the sailboat. Tilly takes it from him and secures it.

"Nice!" Moore says.

"Soup's on!" Zara calls.

They all sit down to a beautiful table with flowers, grilled fish, assorted poke, Hawaiian bread, and tropical fruits.

Spit turns to Moore, sitting next to him. He whispers, "Where's the soup?"

"It's a figure of speech."

Spit holds up two fingers in a peace sign. He puts his other arm around Moore.

"Thanks, buddy. Peace on."

THE END

PEDRO'S PRIMER

Tilly and my pug-buddy, Plastic, asked me to share a few
words with you.
I like two walks every day and to hike with Tilly, where I can
run off-leash and swim in creeks, rivers, and oceans. It makes
me very sad when I see plastic trash in the water. I don't
understand it.
Please drink and eat in reusable dog bowls. When you throw
a plastic bottle, container, or straw in the trash, it ends up in
the ocean where it hurts a lot of fish and also gets back in our
drinking water. Refill, Bill!
Woof!

PEDRO DE SOUSA SARAMAGO MEGELLAN

EXTRA FUN READS!

FREE DOWNLOAD

SHORT STORY PREQUEL

Hip-Hop Hope Slope

aviskalfsbeek.com/free

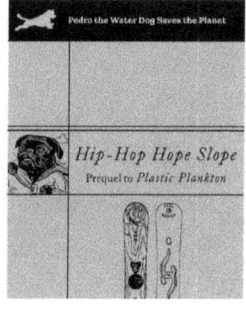

EXTRA EXTRA EARLY
CHAPTERS & BOOKS

FOR EARLY ADVANCES:

Prereleased chapters

Behind the scenes

Pedro planet love

Other writings

patreon.com/pedrothewaterdog

AFTERWORD

"In a perfect world, our waters run healthy, clean, and free. Their waves and their currents and their stillness welcome all of us to heal, play, create, and love abundantly. For many of us, until that moment of observance or submergence, we work hard and struggle to maintain our ancient, personal connection to water. There is an interdependency with the natural world that goes beyond ecosystems, biodiversity, or economic benefits; our neurons and water need each other to live.

All I really want to say is this: Get in the water."

Dr. Wallace J. Nichols, Author of Blue Mind

www.ingramcontent.com/pod-product-compliance
Lightning Source LLC
Chambersburg PA
CBHW071126100726
47908CB00008B/2508